"We have a picnic planned for this Saturday," the pastor said.

"Not only to give potential parents information, but as a meet and greet so the mentors can get to know the boys and vice versa," he continued. "We'll match up the pairs after."

"I don't know," Jake hedged. "I'd have to know more about what's involved."

"It's easy. You just take a kid who needs a little time and attention under your wing."

Under his wing.

That, Jake thought, wasn't as easy as it sounded. Not for someone like him.

Maybe he should have thought it through a little more when he'd told God he'd say *yes* to whatever He asked.

Especially considering he had been about to die when he made the promise.

Books by Kathryn Springer

Love Inspired

Tested by Fire
Her Christmas Wish
By Her Side
For Her Son's Love
A Treasure Worth Keeping
Hidden Treasures
Family Treasures
Jingle Bell Babies
*A Place to Call Home
*Love Finds a Home

*Mirror Lake

Steeple Hill

Front Porch Princess
Hearts Evergreen
  "A Match Made
    for Christmas"
Picket Fence Promises
The Prince Charming List

KATHRYN SPRINGER

is a lifelong Wisconsin resident. Growing up in a "newspaper" family, she spent long hours as a child plunking out stories on her mother's typewriter and hasn't stopped writing since! She loves to write inspirational romance because it allows her to combine her faith in God with her love of a happy ending.

Love Finds a Home
Kathryn Springer

Steeple
Hill®

Published by Steeple Hill Books™

STEEPLE HILL BOOKS

Steeple
Hill®

Recycling programs
for this product may
not exist in your area.

ISBN-13: 978-0-373-81500-5

LOVE FINDS A HOME

www.SteepleHill.com

Printed in U.S.A.

And I pray that you, being rooted and established in love, may have power, together with all the saints, to grasp how wide and long and high and deep is the love of Christ.

—*Ephesians* 3:17–18

To Colleen, my "third" daughter, who has a special place in my life and in my heart. Love ya!

Chapter One

"Flowers?" Police Chief Jake Sutton spotted the enormous bouquet of roses the moment he stepped into the break room, where the officers roosted near the coffee pot before heading out on patrol every morning. "I'm touched, guys, but you shouldn't have."

The three men staring morosely at the fragrant centerpiece snapped to attention at the sound of his voice.

"We didn't," Phil Koenigs muttered, the droop of his narrow shoulders more pronounced than usual.

"No offense, though, Chief," Tony Tripenski added quickly. "We would have brought you flowers if we knew you liked them." His eyes widened when he saw Jake's eyebrow lift. "I mean, not that you look like the type of guy who likes flowers…"

Phil rolled up the fingers on one hand and cuffed Tony on the shoulder. "Put the shovel away, Trip. All you're doing is digging yourself a deeper hole."

Glowering, the younger officer folded his arms across his chest and slumped lower in the chair.

Jake paused long enough to pour himself a cup of coffee before making his way to the table. Something warned him that he was going to need the extra caffeine. The last time he'd seen the men in such a dismal mood was the day he'd officially been sworn in as Mirror Lake's new police chief.

He flipped an empty chair away from the table and straddled it. "If one of you has a secret admirer, you'd look a little happier. That means someone must be in the doghouse with the wife."

"The doghouse would be easier," Steve Patterson, one of the part-time officers, grumbled.

"Yeah." Trip nodded. "*Much* easier. I'd rather face Sherry when she's in a mood than…" His voice dropped to a whisper. "You know who."

No, Jake didn't know. He hadn't been born and raised in the area, something more than a few people had been quick to point out since his arrival.

His gaze cut back to Phil. If he wanted a straight answer, it would most likely come from the senior officer. As second in command, Phil had been the most likely candidate to step into the shoes of the former police chief, who'd opted for an early retirement. Instead, he'd astonished everyone by turning down the position.

Any concern that Phil's decision would make the transfer of power a rocky one had been put to rest when Jake found out Phil was the one who'd pulled his resume from the stack of applications and given it his personal stamp of approval.

He still wasn't quite sure why. But he did know that if it weren't for the dour officer's willingness to fill him in on the local—and sometimes colorful—history of the town and the people who lived there, Jake might still be suffering from an acute case of culture shock. Within the first twenty-four hours, he'd discovered that what Mirror Lake lacked in population, it made up for in quirks.

He had a feeling he was about to add another one to the list.

He glanced at the officer, surprised when Phil averted his gaze. "Phil? Flowers?"

The officer scratched at a coffee stain on the table with his thumbnail. Sighed. "They're for Emma Barlow."

"Okay." Jake drew a blank on the name. "I'll bite. Who is Emma Barlow?"

The three men exchanged looks but none of

them seemed in a hurry to enlighten him. Jake waited, drawing on the patience that had become second nature while working as an undercover narcotics officer.

"Brian Barlow's widow," Phil finally said. "Brian was a good man. A good…cop."

Was.

Jake didn't miss the significance of the word. Or the flash of grief in the older officer's eyes. It was the first time he'd heard about the department losing an officer. Apparently that was one bit of local history Phil hadn't been eager to share.

"What happened?"

"He was killed in the line of duty six years ago. High-speed chase." Steve picked up the story with a sideways glance at Phil, who'd lapsed into silence again. "On the anniversary of his death, one of us takes flowers to his wife…" He caught himself. "I mean his widow."

"That's thoughtful of you." Jake wasn't surprised. From what he'd learned about the town over the past few weeks, an annual tribute to a fallen officer was the kind of thing he'd expect from the tightly knit group of people who lived in Mirror Lake.

No one agreed or disagreed with the statement. But if anything, they looked more miserable than they had when he'd walked in. For the first time,

Jake noticed three plastic straws lined up next to the vase.

Absently, he picked one up and rolled it between his fingers.

The *short* one.

His eyes narrowed but no one noticed. Probably because they'd all found a different focal point in the room to latch on to.

The evidence in front of him and the officers' expressions could only lead Jake to one conclusion.

"Don't tell me that you're drawing straws to see who gets to deliver the flowers?"

"No." Trip almost choked on the word.

Jake might have believed the swift denial if the tips of Trip's ears hadn't turned the same shade of red as his hair.

He turned to Steve and raised an eyebrow.

Steve's Adam's apple convulsed in response. "We draw straws to decide who *has* to deliver them," he muttered.

"Let me get this straight. You buy Emma Barlow flowers every year but no one wants to *give* them to her?"

Absolute silence followed the question. Which, Jake decided, was an answer in itself. Under any circumstances, it was difficult to lose a fellow officer, but in a small community like Mirror

Lake, he guessed it had shaken the town to its very foundation.

He buried a sigh. "I'll drop them off. Where does she live?"

The officers stared at Jake as if he'd just volunteered to walk into a drug deal wearing a wire on the *outside* of his clothes.

"You?" Steve's voice cracked on the word.

Not quite the reaction Jake had expected.

"Is there something I'm missing here?" he asked. "Don't I just knock on the door, express my condolences and give Emma Barlow the flowers?"

Phil opened his mouth to speak but Trip and Steve beat him to it.

"That's pretty much it, Chief." A hopeful look dawned in Trip's eyes.

"Yup." Steve's head bobbed in agreement. "That's all there is to it."

"Phil?"

The officer's fingers drummed an uneven beat against the table. "That's usually the way it goes," he said cautiously.

Usually?

"So you think she would be more comfortable if someone she knew brought them over—" Jake didn't have a chance to finish the sentence. Phil's radio crackled to life as a call came in from dispatch.

The three officers surged to their feet.

"Better go." Phil moved toward the door at an impressive speed, Steve and Trip practically stumbling over his heels in their haste to follow.

"Wait a second." Jake couldn't believe what he was seeing. "It takes all three of you to respond to a *dog* complaint?"

Phil had already disappeared, leaving Steve and Trip glued to the floor as if Jake had aimed a spotlight on them.

"It might be a *big* dog," Trip mumbled.

"Huge." Steve nodded.

"And vicious," Trip added. "You never know."

"That's true." Jake suppressed a smile. "So, in the interest of maintaining public safety, I'll expect a full, *written* report on this large, vicious dog and details of the encounter before you leave today."

The officers' unhappy looks collided in midair.

"Sure, Chief." Trip plucked at his collar. "Not a problem."

He vanished through the doorway but Steve paused for a moment. "Emma Barlow lives in the last house on Stony Ridge Road. It's a dead end off the west side of the lake—"

A hand closed around Steve's arm and yanked him out of sight.

Jake shook his head.

Definitely one for the list.

* * *

Emma Barlow sat at the kitchen table, palms curled around a cup of tea that had cooled off more than an hour ago.

Ordinarily, she could set her clock by the arrival of an officer from the Mirror Lake Police Department. Nine o'clock sharp, as if the stop at her house was the first order of business for the day.

Or something to get over with as quickly as possible.

Sometimes Emma wondered if the officers dreaded August fifteenth as much as she did.

After six years, she knew exactly what to do. As if every moment, every movement, were choreographed.

Emma would open the door and find one of the officers, most likely Phil Koenigs, standing on the porch with a bouquet of red roses.

Always roses.

They didn't speak. Emma preferred it that way. She accepted the flowers more easily than she would have awkward condolences. Or even worse, a pious reminder that God loved her and she should accept Brian's death as His will.

Emma had often wondered why no one else saw the contradiction there. If God really loved her, would He have left her a widow at the age of twenty-four? Wouldn't He have somehow intervened to save Brian?

Those were the kinds of questions that ran through Emma's mind during the sleepless nights following the funeral, but she'd learned not to voice them out loud. It hadn't taken her long to discover that most people, no matter how sympathetic or well-meaning, seemed to give grief a wide berth. As if they were afraid if they got too close, it would touch—or stain—their own lives somehow.

No one liked to be reminded how fragile life could be. Especially another police officer, who looked at her and saw Brian instead. A life cut short.

Maybe that explained why the officers remained poised on the top step, waiting for her to take the flowers. She would then nod politely. Step back into the house. Close the door. Listen for the car to drive away. The roses would be transported to the cemetery and carefully arranged, one by one, in the bronze vase on Brian's grave.

What she really wanted to do was throw them away.

If it weren't for Jeremy, she probably would. Although her ten-year-old son had very few memories of his father, he took both pride and comfort in knowing that an entire community did.

Jeremy had lost enough; Emma wasn't about to take that away from him.

Unlike her, Brian had been born and raised in Mirror Lake. He'd left after graduation, only to return two years later with a degree in Police Science and a gold wedding band on his left hand, a perfect match with the one now tucked away in her jewelry box.

The snap of a car door closing sucked the air from Emma's lungs. Lost in thought, she hadn't heard a car pull up the driveway. Through the panel of lace curtains on the window, Emma caught a glimpse of a light bar on top of the vehicle.

Rising to her feet, she tried to subdue the memories that pushed their way to the surface. Memories of the night she'd fallen asleep on the sofa, waiting for Brian to come home. But instead of her husband, a visibly shaken Phil Koenigs had shown up at the door…

You can do this, Em. Open the door. Take the roses. Nod politely. Close the door.

Her fingers closed around the knob. And her heart stumbled.

It wasn't Phil who stood there, a bouquet of long-stemmed roses pinched in the bend of his arm.

It was a stranger, empty-handed.

"Emma Barlow?"

A stranger who knew her name.

Emma managed a jerky nod. "Y-yes." Her voice sounded as rusty as the screen door she hadn't found time to replace.

"I'm Jake Sutton." He extended his hand. "The new police chief."

Before she knew what was happening, Emma felt the warm press of his fingers as they folded around hers.

She'd heard a rumor about Chief Jansen's upcoming retirement but hadn't realized he'd been replaced yet. Replaced by a man in his midthirties, whose chiseled features and tousled dark hair gave him an edgy look. A faint web of scars etched the blade of his jaw, as pale and delicate as frost on a window. If it weren't for the white dress shirt and badge, he would have looked more like someone who walked the edge of the law, not a man who dedicated his life enforcing it.

Emma pulled her hand away, no longer sure what she should say. Or do.

Jake Sutton had just changed the rules.

Chapter Two

Jake felt Emma Barlow's hand flutter inside his like a butterfly trapped in a jar. Before she yanked it away.

His first thought when the door opened was that he'd gone to the wrong address. The woman standing on the other side was young. Younger than he expected.

Too young to be a widow.

Fast on the heels of that thought came a second. In an instant, Jake knew why the officers let the short straw decide who delivered the flowers. It wasn't the painful reminder of losing a friend and colleague they didn't want to face.

It was Emma Barlow.

He recognized the anger embedded in her grief; flash-frozen like shards of glass in the smoke-blue eyes staring up at him.

She didn't want flowers. Or sympathy.

She wanted him to leave.

It was a shame that Jake rarely did what people wanted—or expected—him to do.

"Do you mind if I come in?"

Instead of answering, Emma Barlow made a strangled sound.

Was that a yes or a no?

Jake took a step forward. She took a step back... and bumped into the person who'd materialized behind her. A boy about ten or eleven years old, with sandy blond hair a shade or two lighter than hers. Eyes an identical shade of blue.

Jake released a slow breath.

No one at the department had mentioned a child.

Steve had said that Brian Barlow had died six years ago. If this was his son, and the boy had to be, given the striking physical resemblance to Emma, he must have lost his father before he started school.

Something twisted in Jake's gut when Emma put a protective hand on the boy's shoulder. He'd gotten used to the suspicious looks cast his way while he worked undercover, hair scraped back in an unkempt ponytail and a gold stud in one earlobe. He'd gotten rid of both after leaving the force, but Emma Barlow's wary expression still unsettled him. Made him feel like the bad guy.

"Jeremy, this is…Chief Sutton." Emma's husky voice stumbled over the words. "Chief Sutton—my son. Jeremy."

Jake extended his hand. "It's nice to meet you."

The boy hung back, his gaze uncertain. "Where are the flowers?"

The question broadsided Jake. If Emma's son had expected him to show up with a dozen roses, he obviously hadn't followed standard protocol.

Okay, God, I thought I was following your orders.

Jake's silent prayer went up with a huff of frustration. Not at God, but at himself. The trouble was, he'd been a cop longer than he'd been a follower of Jesus, so he wasn't always sure he was getting the faith stuff right.

Over the past six months, he'd tried to tune in to what some referred to as "a still, small voice" or a "gentle inner nudge."

His younger brother, Andy, without mentioning names, of course, claimed that if "someone" had a thick skull, God sometimes had to shout to get their attention. And if that "someone" also possessed a thick skin, the "gentle nudge" might feel more like an elbow to the ribs.

Jake had felt that elbow when he'd reached out to steady the vase on the seat beside him at a stop sign on his way to Emma's. He studied the flowers, as if he'd just been given a piece of evidence, but found nothing unusual about a dozen roses mixed with lacy ferns and a few tufts of those little white flowers he couldn't remember the name of. The standard arrangement a woman received for Valentine's Day or an anniversary. To remind her she was loved…

Another jab.

Jake had closed his eyes.

Did a bouquet of red roses honor her husband's memory? Or was the sight of them one more reminder of everything Emma Barlow had lost?

Jake had turned the squad car around and headed for the florist shop.

Once inside, he'd bypassed the cooler filled with pink and blue carnations, ready and waiting to celebrate the next newborn baby, and dodged a display of vases filled with single-stemmed roses, the grab-and-go kind, best offered with an apology.

His foot had snagged the corner of a wooden pallet, almost pitching him headfirst into the sturdy little tree in the corner.

The clerk explained it had been part of a late-summer shipment that hadn't sold because most people planted trees in the spring. A mistake.

Jake had seen it as divine intervention.

Now he wasn't so sure.

"I brought something else this time."

Jeremy ducked his head and Jake waited, hoping the boy's natural curiosity would trump his fear.

Jeremy scraped the toe of his tennis shoe against the porch, sloughing off a blister of loose paint. His voice barely broke above a whisper but Jake heard him.

"What is it?"

Emma resisted the urge to echo the question.

"Come on. I'll show you." Jake Sutton stepped off the porch and strode toward the squad car. Without asking for her permission, Jeremy bounded after him.

Leaving Emma no choice but to follow.

The police chief opened the back door of the vehicle and pulled out a bucket.

Emma blinked.

He *had* brought something else.

A spindly coat rack of a tree with leaves that looked more like pieces of damp crepe paper glued to the drooping branches.

"What's that?" Jeremy's nose wrinkled as he sidled closer.

"This…" Jake anchored the container against one narrow hip and bumped the door shut. "Is an apple tree."

Jeremy gave it a doubtful look. "I think it's dead."

"It'll be good as new once it's planted. All it needs is some water and sunlight." Jake tilted his head. "I was going to offer to dig the hole, but you look strong enough to do it."

He sounded so certain that Jeremy's chin rose. "S-sure."

Before Emma could protest, Jake transferred the bucket to her son's arms. Jeremy's shoulders sagged under the weight, but to her astonishment his eyes glowed with pride when he turned to look at her.

"Should I find a place to plant it, Mom?"

Emma nodded, not trusting her voice. Although they lived in the country, her son shunned the rough-and-tumble antics that most boys his age enthusiastically embraced. Emma knew she was partially responsible for that. After Brian's death, she'd had no choice but to take Jeremy to work with her at the library, where he'd been forced to find quiet things to occupy his time.

By the time he was old enough to pursue some of his own interests, Jeremy had seemed more content to observe things rather than experience them. Emma had been secretly relieved when it looked as if he hadn't inherited his father's love of a challenge. Brian's desire to push the limits had burned like a flame inside him. One that marriage and becoming a father had only tempered, never fully quenched.

Jeremy flashed a shy smile in the man's direction before trudging away, arms wrapped as tight as insulation around the bucket.

Emma couldn't get her feet to move. Or her vocal cords.

She didn't know what to do with an apple tree. Jake Sutton should have brought roses. Never mind that she didn't *like* roses... It was what he was *supposed* to do. And he should be driving away now...not watching her with golden-brown eyes, as calm and measuring as a timber wolf's.

Those eyes locked with hers and Emma had the uneasy feeling he could read her thoughts. "Do you have a shovel handy?"

Afraid of where the question might lead—possibly to Jake Sutton staying longer?—Emma didn't respond.

Unfortunately, Jeremy did. "There's one in the shed," he called over his shoulder, his mood a whole lot more cheerful than hers.

"Good. You find a spot for the tree while your mother and I round one up."

Didn't she have a say in this?

Emma's hands clenched at her side. "That's not necessary, Chief...Sutton." Her mind was still having a difficult time adjusting to the change. Not only in the name but the man himself. "You must be busy. Jeremy and I don't want to keep you from your work."

"It's Jake. And don't worry about me getting into trouble." A glint of humor appeared in his eyes. "I'm the boss."

Said, Emma thought a bit resentfully, with the confidence that police officers seemed to wear as comfortably as their uniform. And if that weren't enough, the amusement bloomed into laughter, causing a chain reaction. It spilled into the creases fanning out from those amber eyes and tugged at the corners of his lips. The result was a charming, if slightly lopsided smile.

He wasn't supposed to smile, either.

Emma tried to ignore her uninvited guest as they made their way around the corner of the house, past the rusted swing set Jeremy had already out-grown. Weeds sprouted at the base of the poles, a reminder that she'd been neglecting the yard work.

She caught a sigh before it escaped.

Not for the first time, she wished there were more hours in the day.

Between working at the library and her respon-sibilities at home, Emma didn't have a lot of time to devote to general maintenance around the property. There had been times when she'd thought about selling the place and leaving Mirror Lake for good...if memories of Brian hadn't become fragile threads that held her there.

And if she'd had somewhere else to go.

She tried to see the property from Jake Sutton's eyes. Did he notice some of the shingles had begun to peel away from the roof like the soles of a worn-out shoe? That dandelions dotted a shaggy backyard in desperate need of a lawn mower?

In spite of his easy stride and that disarming smile, something warned her that the man didn't miss much.

"How about right here, Mom?" Jeremy waved to them from the spot he'd chosen. Smack-dab in the middle of the yard.

Emma looked around, not sure if she wanted it in such a conspicuous spot. Before she had time to respond, Jake nodded.

"Good choice. It'll get full sun there."

Jeremy seemed to grow several inches, basking in Jake Sutton's approval as if *he'd* been the one exposed to sunlight.

It didn't make sense. Her son, ordinarily shy around strangers, was responding to the police chief as if they'd known each other for years.

Emma changed direction, veering toward the shed in search of a shovel. The knot in her stomach loosened when Jake didn't follow her. Facing any critters that might have taken up residence inside was more appealing than facing *him* at the moment.

When she returned a few minutes later, brushing cobwebs from the rusty shovel she'd unearthed, Jake was kneeling beside Jeremy. Heads bowed together, shadow and sun, as they studied the planting directions printed on a ragged piece of paper attached to one of the branches with a piece of twine.

Her lips tightened.

The sooner she started digging, the sooner Jake Sutton would leave them alone.

Emma aimed the shovel at a random spot in the grass but Jake plucked it gently from her grasp. "Jeremy's got it." He aimed a wink in her son's direction, as if the two of them had already discussed how to deal with the possibility of any maternal resistance.

"We haven't had much rain. The ground is pretty hard." She reached for the tool again but Jake handed it to Jeremy, who reacted as if he'd been given the Olympic torch.

Emma worried her bottom lip between her teeth while she watched Jeremy's face scrunch in concentration as he threw his weight against the handle. The ground barely cracked beneath the blade.

"I can—" Emma started to say.

"It's okay, Mom," Jeremy gasped. "I got it."

"You're doing great." Jake smiled again. At *her*. As if he knew how difficult it was not to take over. To watch Jeremy struggle.

The next five minutes seemed like an hour. Finally Jake stepped forward. "Looks great, Jeremy. Why don't you take the tree out of the bucket while I clear some of this loose dirt out of the hole?"

"Okay," Jeremy panted the word, relinquishing the shovel with a grin.

Emma felt something shift inside her. She had a feeling that by the time Jake cleared some of the "loose dirt" out of the hole, it would be deep enough to plant the root ball.

Jeremy wrestled the apple tree out of the bucket, and together he and Jake dropped it carefully into the hole.

If possible, the sapling looked even more forlorn than it had in the bucket.

Jeremy must have thought so, too. "I'm going to get some water."

He scampered away, leaving Emma alone with Jake Sutton.

"I hope you don't mind." The rough velvet of

his voice scraped across Emma's frayed emotions. "I thought you might like a change this year. Something that will last longer than a vase of flowers."

Change?

Emma almost laughed.

She'd been through enough changes to last a lifetime.

Chapter Three

"So, how are you adjusting to small-town life?" Matthew Wilde slid into the booth opposite Jake.

"Did we have an appointment?" Jake feigned confusion. "Because I'm pretty sure I wouldn't choose to answer that question during the morning rush at the Grapevine Café."

"I don't wait for my congregation to make appointments." The pastor shrugged. "I've discovered it's more effective to go where they are. Like Jesus did."

"Mmm. That explains why you spend so much time out on the lake."

"Jesus did say something about becoming fishers of men." Matt grinned. "What better place to find them?"

"What can I get you, Pastor?" Kate Nichols, the owner of the café, appeared beside their table, her smile as vibrant as the auburn curls that poked out like rusty bedsprings under the yellow bandana she wore.

"Just coffee."

Kate propped one hand on her hip. "You know as well as I do that as soon as I leave you're going to change your mind and want the special with a side of hash browns and bacon. Why don't you save me the trouble and put the order in now?"

"I'm surprised you stay in business, Kate. The way you treat your customers. And your pastor," Matt added piously.

Kate arched a brow. "Eggs?"

"Over medium."

She turned to Jake. "Chief?"

"Just coffee, thanks."

Kate tucked the pen in her apron pocket and flitted away. She reminded Jake of a humming-bird. Always in motion. From what he'd heard, Kate Nichols was Mirror Lake's own five-foot-two generator, keeping the town running.

"Why did she believe you and not me?" Matt complained.

"I never change my mind."

The vinyl booth crackled as Matt leaned back and folded his arms behind his head. "Your name came up yesterday."

"Let me guess. Delia Peake." From the way the

woman had glared at him from the back row of the choir on Sunday morning, Jake guessed she was still steamed that the animal who'd trampled her garden and sampled the produce as if it were a buffet had eluded capture. As far as Delia was concerned, if Jake was worth his salt as a police chief, he would have apprehended the furry little vandal himself. Never mind that he'd been out at the Barlow house at the time of the "attack."

Jake jerked his thoughts back into line as they strayed to Emma Barlow. Again. Almost a week had gone by since he'd tossed protocol out of the window and presented her with an apple tree instead of a bouquet of roses. The memory of that morning should have started to fade. Instead, the opposite had occurred. Jake found himself thinking about it—about *her*—even more. Emma Barlow had a way of sneaking into his thoughts before he realized what was happening…

Like right now.

"No, it wasn't Delia. This time." From the amusement lurking in Matt's eyes, Jake knew the pastor had heard about the garden fiasco. "A few months ago, Harold Davis, one of the church elders, met with me about starting a mentoring program. Matching men from the congregation with boys from single-parent families in town. The initial feedback from everyone was positive, so we researched the success of similar programs in other churches and wrote up a mission statement. I've been compiling a list of men willing to serve as positive role models for boys who don't have one in their lives."

Jake could see where this was going. "And you want to add mine to the list."

"I already did."

"This is where I remind you that I'm new to the area. You don't know anything about me." Only what Jake had told the pastor the first time they'd met, and he'd deliberately left out a few details of his former life.

"I know the important things." Matt's gaze remained level. "You're a believer. You're growing in your relationship with Christ. And you mentioned that you wanted to get involved in one of the ministries at Church of the Pines."

Jake could have argued every point. He was a *new* believer. He had a long way to go when it came to relationships, not only with the Lord but with everyone in general. And he'd had no idea that a casual comment about serving in the church would bring about such quick results. Jake had meant it, but thought he would have more time to prepare for the task. Like a few months. Or years.

"Has anyone ever told you that you're awfully pushy for a preacher?"

"Can't honestly say I've heard that one," Matt denied cheerfully.

"Only because people won't say it to his face," Kate interrupted. She slid a steaming plate in front of the pastor and checked the level on Jake's coffee cup before moving to the next table.

"We have a picnic planned for this coming Saturday," Matt went on. "Not only to give potential parents information but as a meet and greet so the mentors can get to know the boys and vice versa. We'll match up the pairs after that."

"I don't know," Jake hedged. "I would have to know more about what's involved."

"It's easy. You just take a kid who needs a little time and attention under your wing."

Under his wing.

That, Jake thought, wasn't as easy as it sounded. Not for someone like him, anyway. Not too long ago, the only thing he could claim to have "under his wing" was his duty weapon.

Maybe he should have thought it through a little more when he'd told God he would say "yes" to whatever He asked.

Especially considering that he *had* been about to die when he'd made the promise.

* * *

"Listen, Mom! Do you hear that?" Jeremy's head popped out from behind the colorful screen that separated the children's area from the rest of the library.

He had volunteered to reorganize the picture-book section, literally turned upside down by a rambunctious pair of four-year-old twin boys who had visited the library with their teenage babysitter earlier that morning.

Emma didn't bother to tap her finger against her lips, a gentle reminder for her son to keep his voice down. For the past two hours, they had been the only ones in the building.

"Hear what?" She tipped her head, pretending to be unaware of the faint but unmistakable sound of music drifting through the open windows.

"The ice-cream truck." Jeremy abandoned his post and rushed toward her. "Can I get something? Please?"

Emma was already reaching for her purse, stashed on the bottom shelf of the circulation desk. Apparently Charlie "The Ice-Cream Man" Pendleton had decided to take advantage of another hot August afternoon. His ancient truck, with its equally ancient sound system, drew children into the streets with an enthusiasm that transformed the local Christmas tree farmer into a Pied Piper in denim bib overalls.

The music grew louder, a sure sign that the ice-cream truck had just turned the corner as it cruised toward its destination—a shady spot in front of the Grapevine Café.

"Here you go." Emma handed him some change. "Be careful when you cross the street."

Jeremy stuffed the money into the front pocket of his khaki shorts. "I will."

"And remember not to go any farther than the café."

"I won't."

He'll be fine, Emma told herself as the heavy door swung shut behind him.

Charlie Pendleton didn't have a lot to say but below the dusty brim of the man's faded cap were eyes as sharp and watchful as a school crossing guard. Not to mention that his first stop was located kitty-corner to the police station…

Emma's heart dipped as an image of Jake Sutton flashed in her mind. And she didn't appreciate him intruding on her thoughts like this, any more than she had his unexpected appearance on her doorstep.

Although he had left a few minutes after Jeremy had returned with the bucket of water for the apple tree, his departure hadn't given Emma much relief.

Because for some reason, Jake Sutton had become Jeremy's favorite topic of conversation over the past few days.

He hadn't even been disappointed that there were no flowers to take to the cemetery. Jake's unexpected but creative gesture had impacted Jeremy in a way that Emma hadn't anticipated.

It had impacted her, too, but not in the same way.

From what she had seen, Jake didn't seem to care about things like rules or expectations or even simple protocol, for that matter. He reminded her of the timber wolves that had been introduced into the heavily wooded northern counties, but gradually migrated into more populated areas, unmindful of any boundaries, natural or man-made. Not necessarily dangerous, but unpredictable.

Only Emma didn't *want* unpredictable. Not anymore.

On his way back to the department, Jake spotted Charlie Pendleton's truck parked in front of the Grapevine Café. Unlike his route, the man's appearance in town never followed a set pattern or schedule.

The ice-cream truck had rattled through town on several occasions, each time pulling Jake into a surreal Mayberry moment. A year ago, Jake wouldn't have believed that a town like Mirror Lake actually existed.

Or that he would be living there.

He slowed down as he got closer and noticed a group of larger, middle-school-age boys push their way through the children patiently waiting to place their order. Jake recognized them immediately. Too young to get jobs and yet too old for babysitters, the boys' favorite pastime seemed to be hanging out at the park or getting into mischief.

By the time Jake pulled over and hopped out of the squad car, they had formed a tight circle around someone at the back of the line.

One of them spotted Jake and sank his elbow into his friend's side.

"Hey…" The boy's voice snapped off when he saw Jake walking purposefully toward them.

The circle parted immediately, giving Jake a clear view of the unlucky kid who had been trapped inside.

Jeremy Barlow.

The boy looked more worried than hurt, but Jake's protective instincts—instincts he hadn't known that he possessed until now—kicked into high gear.

"What's going on?" He turned his attention to the largest boy in the group.

"Nothing. We're just goofing around." As if to

prove his point, he gave Jeremy a friendly cuff on the shoulder.

Jeremy winced but remained silent. Jake stepped between them, forcing the others to fall back. "Doesn't Charlie have a rule that the youngest kids get to go to the front of the line?"

"Yeah, but it's stupid," one of the boys muttered. "It should be whoever gets here first."

"If that's the case, then from what I saw Jeremy would still be ahead of you." Jake folded his arms. "Right?"

The oldest boy looked as if he were going to argue the point when Charlie's voice, as crackly as the speakers, broke through the hum of chatter around them.

"Okay, that's it! There are kids waiting for me at the next stop." The elderly man closed up the back of the truck and jumped inside, deaf to the chorus of protests that rose from the boys who had been harassing Jeremy.

Jake's eyes narrowed. "You can go. But at the next stop, I'm going to assume you'll go to the end of the line and there won't be any more 'goofing around.'"

Mumbling their agreement, the boys made a beeline for the pile of bicycles on the sidewalk in front of the café.

The rest of the children began to disperse.

Jeremy's pensive gaze followed the truck as it chugged away.

"Are you going to catch up with him at the park?" Jake asked, knowing it was the second stop on Charlie's route.

He shook his head. "Mom doesn't want me to go farther than the café."

Jake frowned. When he was Jeremy's age, he and his best friend had practically worn the rubber off their bicycle tires on summer afternoons like this. His mother had seemed to accept the nomadic lifestyle of adolescent boys. Her only rule was that Jake eat breakfast before he left the house in the morning and be back in time for supper. And what happened during the hours in between he didn't need to account for.

Given the way Emma had hovered close to Jeremy the first time they'd met, Jake had a hunch she wasn't as lenient.

"Mom is still at the library. I should go back." Jeremy squared his thin shoulders.

Jake couldn't help but be moved by the boy's valiant attempt to hide his disappointment. "Do you want a ride?" he heard himself say.

The blue eyes widened. "In the police car?"

"That's what I'm driving." Jake couldn't help but smile at his reaction. "Hop in."

Jeremy didn't have to be told twice. He was

sitting in the passenger seat with his seat belt buck-led before Jake opened the driver's side door.

"My dad drove a car like this, didn't he?"

The innocent question took Jake off guard. Did Jeremy remember his father? "I'm sure it was simi-lar," he said carefully. "But it probably didn't have a laptop like this one."

"It's important to keep up with changes in technology," Jeremy said seriously as he leaned forward to study the radar gun mounted to the dash.

"That's right." Jake's lips twitched as he turned the car around. "How is the apple tree doing?"

"I think it's going to live. And it's better than flowers, even if we didn't have anything to take to the cemetery."

Jake's hands tightened on the steering wheel. He hadn't considered that the bouquet the police department gave Emma would end up on Brian's grave.

Further proof that he'd made a mistake.

"There's Mom." Jeremy pointed out the window.

Emma stood on the sidewalk in front of the library, her willowy figure accentuated by the white blouse and knee-length denim skirt she wore. Her gaze was riveted on the squad car.

The expression on her face warned Jake that he'd just made another mistake.

The sight of a squad car cruising down the street caused Emma's hands to clench at her sides. It was silly, she knew, to have such a strong reaction to a vehicle.

She steeled herself, waiting for it to go past. Instead, the car glided to a stop in front of the library.

The sight of a familiar face in the window squeezed the air from her lungs.

What happened?

The words stuck in Emma's throat as she watched Jake Sutton's lean frame unfold from the vehicle. He prowled around to the passenger side and opened the door.

"Chief Sutton gave me a ride in the squad car, Mom." Jeremy was smiling as he jumped out. "It's pretty sweet."

"But…" Emma struggled to find her voice. "What about the ice cream? Didn't you catch up to Charlie in time?"

The smile faded. "Yeah."

Emma sensed there was more to the story and her heart sank. "Was someone bothering you again?"

"You know Brad and his friends. They just like to show off," Jeremy mumbled.

She glanced at Jake and found him regarding her with that measuring look. The one that made her want to run for cover.

"Everything is fine," he said. "Jeremy mentioned you were at the library, so I offered to give him a ride back."

"And he let me turn on the lights." Jeremy's smile returned.

Emma caught her breath as a memory surfaced, momentarily breaking through the grief that had formed like a crust of ice over her heart.

On Brian's official first day with the Mirror Lake police department, he had stopped home and handed her a camera, shamelessly turning his lunch break into a twenty-minute photo session. His attempt to strike a serious pose had made Emma laugh—which had sparked Brian's laughter in return.

Every one of those moments had been captured in heartbreaking detail except for one difference.

That carefree young woman was someone Emma no longer recognized. Someone who no longer existed.

Watching Emma's eyes darken, Jake realized he'd done more than cross a line. He'd inadvertently stirred up something in her past. It was possible that in order to cope, Emma had found it easier to tend her grief instead of her memories.

"Mom?" Jeremy tugged on her arm. "It's got a really great computer, too. They can look up all kind of things. I'm not in it, though, so we looked up you instead."

Jake winced as Emma snapped back to the present and turned on him.

"Me?"

Jake smiled, hoping she would realize that running her name through the system had been a harmless illustration to satisfy Jeremy's curiosity, not an invasion of her privacy. "Date of birth March fifteenth. And you have a very clean driving record."

Emma took a step back. "Jeremy, it's time to go. I have to lock up now."

The message in her blue eyes was clear.

If Emma had her way, that was all he would know about her.

Chapter Four

Emma was up to her wrists in wet cement when her cell phone rang. She managed to dry off her hands and wrestle the phone from the pocket of her jeans on the fourth ring, seconds before the call went to voice mail.

"Hello?"

"Mrs. Barlow? This is Pastor Wilde from Church of the Pines."

Emma's fingers tightened on the phone.

She should have expected this. Jeremy had been drawn into the church's fold by a colorful flyer he'd seen stapled to the bulletin board at the library, advertising a special weeklong children's program. Emma had agreed to let him participate, assuming her son's interest would end once the seven days were over. She hadn't considered that Jeremy would want to start attending the worship services, but at his insistence they'd gone to Church of the Pines the past few Sundays.

For his sake, she'd endured the sermons that reminded her God loved her, and smiled politely at people while keeping a careful distance. But while Emma had ignored the little white cards the ushers handed out, asking for the name, address and phone number of visitors, she remembered that Jeremy had diligently filled one out each time.

Emma looked at the pieces of colored glass scattered on her work table, silently calculating how much time she had before the mixture began to set up.

"I'm right in the middle of something…" She paused, hoping the pastor would take the hint.

"When would be a good time to call back?"

The pleasant voice remained cheerful but firm, letting Emma know that her hesitance was only prolonging the inevitable. "I suppose I have a few minutes right now. What is it you wanted to talk about?"

"I'm calling people to let them know about the mentoring ministry picnic on Saturday afternoon. It starts at noon—"

"Mentoring ministry?" Emma knew it wasn't polite to interrupt but she couldn't prevent the words from spilling out. "I'm sorry, but I'm not sure what you're talking about, Pastor Wilde." And the last thing she wanted to do was get involved with Church of the Pines. Sitting through the Sunday morning services was proving difficult enough.

A moment of silence followed. "I'm sorry, Mrs. Barlow." Pastor Wilde sounded a little confused. "There was a short write-up in the bulletin this past Sunday. Local boys from single-parent families are matched with men from the congregation who commit to spending several hours a week with them. It can be helping with homework, grabbing a burger or shooting hoops together. Whatever the pair decides to do. My job as the coordinator is to pray for any specific needs they might have and oversee the group activities once a month."

Single-parent families.

There it was. No matter how hard she tried to be both mom and dad to Jeremy—to meet all his needs—their home fell into that category. It didn't matter that they hadn't had a choice. That Brian's death had pushed them there.

"I doubt that Jeremy would be interested. He's very shy and wouldn't be comfortable meeting with someone he doesn't know." *And neither would I,* Emma added silently.

Pastor Wilde cleared his throat. "Ah, Jeremy is interested, Mrs. Barlow. In fact, he turned in a registration form already."

The phone almost slipped through Emma's fingers. "Are you sure it was Jeremy? Maybe it was his Sunday school teacher. Or another adult."

Emma heard the sound of papers rustling.

"I'm, ah, looking at his signature right now."

She released a quiet breath, unwilling to believe that Jeremy had signed up on his own. One of the older boys must have decided to play a practical joke on her introverted son. It wouldn't be the first time. "I'll talk to Jeremy. Thank you for calling."

"Mrs. Barlow?" Pastor Wilde must have sensed she was about to hang up. "Attending the picnic on Saturday doesn't mean Jeremy is obligated to join the program. Abby Porter offered to host the picnic at Mirror Lake Lodge and there will be an informal question-and-answer time after lunch.

"I should add that I've personally met with all the prospective mentors and they've had extensive background checks done. It's a blessing we've got men who are willing to donate their time and energy to be positive role models."

Positive role models to boys without fathers.

"It sounds like a good idea," Emma murmured.

For someone else's child.

She couldn't imagine letting Jeremy spend time

with someone she didn't know, background check or not.

"Then we'll see you and Jeremy on Saturday?"

"I'll think about it."

Emma hung up the phone. At least she hadn't lied. She did think about it.

And the answer was no.

Why had she said yes?

Emma took one look at the people milling around the immaculate, beautifully landscaped lawn and almost turned the car around.

She glanced at Jeremy, who was already wrestling his seat belt off. Her son's eager expression answered the question.

After that disturbing phone call from Pastor Wilde, Emma had waited until dinnertime to bring up the subject of the mentoring ministry, still convinced there had been a mistake—that someone else had turned in the registration form with her son's name on it.

Jeremy's whoop of excitement, however, had immediately proved Emma's theory wrong. She hadn't been prepared for his enthusiasm when he learned about the pastor's invitation to the picnic… or his reaction when she told him they wouldn't be able to go.

Emma winced at the memory.

He'd been crushed.

So Emma had explained—quite patiently she'd thought—the reasons why she didn't think that being involved in the mentoring program was a good idea.

Jeremy had listened. And then her quiet, sensitive little boy had leaned forward, looked her straight in the eye and suggested a compromise.

A compromise!

"Mom, you're always telling me that it isn't a good idea to jump to conclusions, right? That a person should do some research before making a decision. I think we should go to the picnic and find out the facts. If you decide you don't want me to do it, then I'll be okay with that."

How could she argue? Especially since it was obvious which member of the Barlow family was guilty of "jumping to conclusions" this time!

The request was fair. Reasonable. But now, watching a group of preadolescent boys zigzag across the lawn in hot pursuit of the one carrying a football, Emma was convinced she'd made a mistake.

"Jeremy—" The car door snapped the sentence in half.

Tension curled in Emma's stomach.

There was no turning back now. Not only had

Jeremy escaped, but Abby Porter had spotted their car and was making her way across the yard.

Somehow, the innkeeper managed to look stunning in faded jeans and a pale green T-shirt that matched her eyes. With her blond hair pulled back in a casual knot and a colorful apron tied around her waist, Abby looked far different from the sophisticated woman in velvet and pearls who had appeared in the ad campaigns for her family's elite hotel chain in years past.

Emma, who'd chosen to wear a navy twill skirt and white blouse, felt positively dowdy by comparison.

"Emma!" Abby appeared at the window. "I'm so glad you're here."

Emma wished she could say the same. She slid out of the driver's seat, resisting the urge to dive back inside the vehicle. Abby immediately linked arms with her, almost as if the other woman had read her mind.

"The turnout this afternoon is higher than we expected." Abby smiled. "I'm glad Pastor Wilde and Harold Davis realized there was a need for something like this in our community."

The need for boys to have male role models in their lives.

The reminder scraped against Emma's soul. She was doing her best to raise Jeremy. He was all she had left in the world. After Brian's death, her son's presence had warmed her heart like a tiny flame, keeping her emotions from growing cold. Over the years, Emma had tried to make sure Jeremy didn't feel as if he were missing out on something, and yet now he wanted to spend time with a mentor.

A *stranger*.

"I'm not sure it's the right thing for Jeremy," Emma said stiffly. She didn't want to offend Abby but she needed to make it clear that she hadn't made a decision whether or not he could join the program.

"Then I'm glad you came to check it out." Abby didn't look the least bit ruffled by her honesty. "And I've been hoping for a chance to talk to you. One of my guests asked for your business card last weekend."

"I don't have a business card," Emma murmured, trying to keep track of Jeremy as he bounded ahead of them.

Abby gave her a playful nudge. "I know you don't, silly. That was a hint."

"The number for the library is in the phone book."

Abby's laughter caused several heads to swivel in their direction. "You're so funny, Emma. And humble, too. I'm not talking about the library. Gloria Rogers saw the mosaic table in my perennial garden and she couldn't stop raving about it. Of course—" Abby's smile turned impish "—I might have mentioned that even though Mirror Lake Lodge has an exclusive contract with the extremely gifted artist who crafted the piece, you might be persuaded to take on more commissions."

"Abby!" Emma didn't bother to hide her shock. "It's a *hobby,* something to pass the time. It's not a business. I already have a job."

Abby looked smug rather than repentant. "That's exactly what I thought when I was sneaking into the hotel kitchen at midnight to make raspberry lemon tarts." She made a sweeping gesture with one arm that encompassed the refurbished lodge and cabins. "Look where that 'little hobby' took me."

But, Emma wanted to argue, that was different. Raspberry lemon tarts were *meant* to be shared. The mosaics she created had sprung from a need to fill long hours and hold painful memories at bay. And like her grief, she'd tried to keep that part of her life private. But in a town as small as Mirror Lake, word had gotten out.

"You can't compare what we do," Emma murmured. "You have a business degree. Experience. I don't have any formal training."

"You have a gift." Abby's tone left no room for

argument. "And when God gives you a gift, it's part of His plan."

Doubt flared from the embers of Emma's grief, snuffing out the unexpected flicker of longing that Abby's words stirred in her heart. There had been a time in her life when she had believed it—before she began to wonder why, when it came to her, did God seem to take away more than He gave?

When she'd met Brian, he had swept her off her feet. She had become a wife at nineteen. A mother at twenty. But Emma's dreams had encompassed a lifetime. They would make a home. Raise a family. Grow old together.

And then she'd lost him.

If all that had been part of God's plan, it seemed safer to keep her distance from Him, too.

"Why don't you and Jeremy find a table and I'll get you both a glass of fresh-squeezed lemonade?" Abby offered.

"All right." Emma looked around but there was no sign of Jeremy. Anywhere. "I don't see him."

"He must have found someone to play with," Abby said.

"Jeremy doesn't care for sports." And was often teased because of it. Tension cinched the muscles between Emma's shoulder blades as she scanned the faces around her.

"Maybe he went down by the lake. Some of the boys were fishing from the dock earlier."

Abby's words, meant to calm her fears, had just the opposite effect. "Jeremy doesn't know how to swim."

Emma felt a pang of guilt at the quickly veiled surprise she saw reflected in Abby's green eyes. She knew what the other woman was thinking. What parent, who lived in a town built on the shore of a lake, wouldn't insist that their child learn to swim?

Emma tried to swallow the knot of panic forming in her throat as Abby gave her arm a comforting squeeze. "I have an idea," she said. "There isn't a boy—or man, for that matter—who will ignore the sound of a dinner bell. I'll give it a ring and I guarantee that you won't have to find Jeremy— he'll find you."

"Thank you." Emma gave Abby a grateful look but didn't wait to see if her idea would work.

She headed down to the lake.

Jake heard the clang of a bell, rallying the troops for lunch, and knew he was running out of time.

The team of mentors would be introduced right after Abby served the meal. If he wanted to let Matt know that he would be more comfortable volunteering in another area of the ministry, he had to do it soon.

Jake had come to the conclusion that he wasn't mentor material only minutes after he'd shown up for the picnic. He had rusty social skills and rough edges his newfound faith hadn't had time to hone. And to top it off, he didn't know a thing about kids. Call him crazy, but wasn't being able to relate to kids an important qualification when it came to being a mentor?

He had taken a walk down the shoreline to think. And to pray.

You know I'm willing, Lord, but I don't think I'm cut out for this. Guys like Matt are better at it. Kids love him—I'd probably scare them away. You must have something else in mind for me, so let me know what it is and I'll do it.

Maybe the prayer team could use another volunteer. He had as much experience in that area as he did interacting with kids, but at least the chance of doing any significant damage remained smaller.

As Jake turned to go back to the lodge, a movement farther down the shoreline caught his attention. He paused, wondering if the flash of color had been a red-winged blackbird searching the cattails for something to eat.

Until he heard a splash.

Knowing how mischievous boys could be, Jake

doubted that Matt had given them free rein of the premises for the picnic. The pastor and Quinn O'Halloran, a local businessman and member of the congregation, had planned a variety of games, part of an ingenious strategy for deterring them from creating their own entertainment.

If it *were* boys from the picnic who'd wandered out of sight.

Off duty or not, Jake had no choice but to check it out. He'd received several complaints earlier in the week from some of the local fishermen, who claimed their vehicles had been broken into while parked at the boat landing. Jake couldn't prove it—yet—but he had a sneaking suspicion that whoever was responsible for breaking into the summer cabins had decided to broaden the playing field.

Jake bypassed the trail and created his own route, one running parallel to the marked hiking path that curved around the lake. As he reached the shore, he saw a boy standing knee-deep in the water, tugging on a rope attached to a makeshift raft bobbing in the waves. He was in no immediate danger that Jake could see, but because the kid's frame looked as thin as one of the reeds growing along the shoreline, Jake decided to lend a hand.

"Hold on!"

At the sound of Jake's voice, the boy turned to look at him.

Jake, who'd always prided himself on keeping his emotions in check, felt his jaw drop in disbelief.

There was no mistaking that pair of serious blue eyes and unruly hank of sandy blond hair.

Jeremy Barlow looked just as astonished to see him. "Chief S-Sutton."

Chapter Five

Without a second thought, Jake kicked off his shoes and waded into the water. Together, they began to pull the raft into the shallows.

"Thanks," Jeremy gasped.

"Does this belong to you?"

Jeremy shook his head, spraying Jake with droplets of lake water. "I saw it floating out there. I was afraid a boat might hit it."

That answered one of his questions. But Jake had another, more important, one. "What are you doing down here by yourself?"

"I'm not by myself," Jeremy said quickly. "I'm with my mom."

"Really?" Jake refused to give in to the sudden urge to look around and see if there was another familiar face close by. A familiar face dominated by smoke-blue eyes and hair the pale golden-brown of winter wheat. "Where is she?"

"She's, um, talking to Miss Porter. At the lodge."

So Emma and Jeremy hadn't come to Mirror Lake Lodge for the picnic. That shouldn't have come as a surprise. Emma was as protective as a mama bear with a cub. Jake couldn't imagine she would trust her son's care to someone else, even for a few hours.

Especially someone like you, an inner voice mocked.

Jake couldn't argue with that. Emma had managed to express her opinion of him the day they'd met without saying a single word. And it wasn't, he reminded himself, as if being Jeremy's mentor was even an option.

Prayer team, remember?

But that didn't mean he was going to leave Jeremy alone by the water. "Does she know you're down here?"

The guilty look on Jeremy's face said it all. "I didn't mean to go this far."

"I'll tell you what—I'll walk back there with you."

His officers might question his sanity, but the thought of seeing Emma again actually lightened Jake's mood. Although given her response when he'd brought Jeremy back in the squad car, he doubted she would be anxious to see *him* again.

"Thanks." Jeremy bit his lip as he looked down at his shorts. "I don't think I was supposed to get wet, either."

"The sun is shining. You'll air-dry in no time," Jake said lightly. "And though I appreciate the fact that you fished this thing out of the lake, the next time—"

"Look!" Jeremy let go of the rope, his startled cry interrupting Jake's lecture on water and the "buddy system." He pointed to a black canvas bag riding along the bottom. As the raft had bumped along the rocks, the bag had ripped open, leaving a trail of tools in the water.

Jeremy began to collect them while Jake hauled the bag onto shore to examine it more closely. He frowned when he saw the name FIELDING stamped on the side of the fabric. Rich Fielding had been one of the people whose cabins had been broken into.

Jeremy knelt beside him, clutching a hammer and wrench against his damp T-shirt. His eyes widened when he read the name on the bag. "I know Mr. Fielding. He teaches science at my school."

"Well, I guarantee he's going to be happy to have his property returned."

"You mean this stuff was stolen?"

"That's right." Jake lifted one side of the raft and

looked underneath it to see if they'd missed anything. "You have pretty good detective skills."

"Really?" Jeremy's eyes shone with the same pride Jake had seen when he'd let him dig the hole for the apple tree.

Jake didn't have an opportunity to answer because Emma burst into view.

"Jeremy Brian Barlow!"

Emma's gaze locked on the boy standing at the edge of the water. At the moment, she wasn't sure whether to scold him or hug him. Or both.

"What are you doing down here?" The panic that had fueled her frantic search drained away, leaving her weak with relief. As Emma took a step forward, the wet sand gave way beneath her feet. She would have stumbled if a hand hadn't shot out to steady her.

"Careful."

Emma's head jerked up. Her relief at finding Jeremy safe and sound was so great, she had barely spared a glance at the man standing a few feet away from him.

Not that Jake Sutton was easy to overlook. Both times Emma had seen the police chief, he'd been in uniform. Today he wore plainclothes suitable for a Saturday afternoon picnic, but the faded jeans and black T-shirt only accentuated the man's rugged, almost untamed, good looks.

For some inexplicable reason, the touch of his hand sowed goose bumps up her arm.

What was he doing here, of all places?

Emma pulled away and turned toward her son. "You know the rules, honey." She wasn't sure if the crackle in her voice was the aftershock of relief from finding Jeremy, or because the warm imprint of Jake's fingers lingered on her skin. "You're supposed to ask for permission if you want to go somewhere."

"I found Mr. Fielding's tools, Mom," Jeremy said. "Someone hid them under the raft. Chief Sutton said I have good detective skills."

"You went out on a *raft?*" Emma directed the question at Jeremy but cut an accusing look at Jake.

"Not in it, Mom," Jeremy said. "I pulled it out."

"It was in the shallow water. Jeremy wasn't in any danger," Jake interjected quietly.

Emma turned back to Jeremy, hoping Jake Sutton would take the hint that this matter was between her and her son. "You have to be careful by the water," she reminded him, all too aware that Jake could hear every word.

"I know." Jeremy released a gusty sigh as he

pulled on his socks and tennis shoes, a reminder that he'd heard this particular lecture before. "But if I knew how to swim, you wouldn't have to worry so much."

Emma felt the weight of Jake's gaze and her cheeks flamed. She wasn't about to explain that it was impossible to teach her son something that she didn't know how to do.

That responsibility should have fallen to Brian. After all, her husband had loved to brag about how much time he and his friends spent in the lake every summer.

One of the high-school athletic coaches offered lessons at the beach every summer, but Emma's job prevented her from leaving to transport Jeremy there and back—and she was hesitant to trust someone she didn't know with his safety.

Discouragement settled over her, the weight of it all too familiar. "We should get back to the lodge." And away from the censure Emma was afraid she would see in those amber eyes. "I'm sure everyone has started eating lunch already."

Emma hoped the thought of food would divert Jeremy's attention. Over the summer, his appetite had increased to the point where she'd started to wonder where he was putting it all. But instead of charging toward the lodge, Jeremy turned a hopeful look toward the very man Emma wanted to get away from.

"Aren't you coming, Chief Sutton?"

She stifled a groan. From what Jake had said, Emma assumed he and Jeremy had met by accident. She hadn't considered he might be a guest at the picnic.

Relief poured through her when Jake shook his head.

"I'm on my way back to the station." He must have seen the disappointment on Jeremy's face because he knelt down until they were eye to eye. "But I'll tell you what. How about we go with 'Chief Sutton' when we're out in public, but if it's just the three of us, you can call me Jake. Is that a deal?"

Jeremy grinned. "It's a deal."

"But only if that's okay with your mom." Jake looked at her. "Emma?"

Why, she wondered in frustration, did Jake Sutton have to have such an attractive voice? The rich timbre washed over her, stirring her senses like the jazz she played on the radio while working on a mosaic.

"I suppose." Emma saw no point making a fuss about it. She couldn't think of any occasion where it would be just the three of them.

The thought should have been accompanied by

relief, but the emotion that skittered through Emma felt, strangely enough, like...disappointment.

Jake watched Emma stumble in the sand again, only this time in her haste to get away from him.
You charmer, you.
Not that he'd *tried* to charm her. Jake was as out of practice at that particular skill as he was at making polite conversation over a glass of lemonade. Fortunately, what he did know how to do was diffuse a tense situation. And Emma had been strung as tight as a new bow when she'd discovered Jeremy by the lake.

Her panic may have faded, but she obviously hadn't changed her opinion of him. She'd barely been able to make eye contact. And when Jake had taken hold of her arm, she had reacted as if he'd burned her.

What did Emma see when she looked at him? Did she see a man or a badge? Was he a person or the symbol of a career that had robbed her of a husband?

The thought chafed.

When he'd asked Phil about Emma after delivering the apple tree, the older officer had still been reluctant to talk about what happened. Jake had pressed a little, asking if Emma had changed after Brian died.

"Can't say for sure." Phil had looked troubled by the question. *"Brian grew up in Mirror Lake. He was an outgoing guy. Liked to be in the middle of things. Emma stayed close to home, especially after Jeremy came along. She wasn't from around here, so no one really got to know her."*

Or no one had tried. Which meant that Emma, a young mother, had been alone in her grief. From what he could see, it still held her locked in a cold grip.

Lord, you can get into the places people shut off from everyone else. You did it for me and I know you can do the same thing for Emma.

That Jake even thought to pray for Emma confirmed the change in *his* heart.

"There you are."

Jake looked up and saw Matt striding down the trail toward him.

"I've been looking for you." Relief surged through Jake and he silently thanked God for giving him the opportunity to let the pastor know that he'd decided against being a mentor.

"That's funny, because I was sent to find *you*." Matt grinned. "Rounding up strays comes with the job."

"Duty calls." Jake jerked his head at the tool bag. "These were stolen from one of the cabins last month."

"Hey, this is your day off," Matt reminded him, a teasing glint in his eyes. "You weren't supposed to be investigating anything more serious than the dessert table."

"Says the man who also chose a career that keeps him on call 24/7."

"Touché." Matt rolled his eyes. "So now what?"

"Steve Patterson is working the day shift. I'll give him a call and have him meet me at the department with the stolen property."

"You're going to miss the meeting." It wasn't a question.

"I'm afraid so." Jake hesitated, torn between not wanting to disappoint the pastor and knowing that the sooner he got this over with, the sooner Matt could look for someone to take his place.

Matt slanted a knowing look at him. "You're having second thoughts, aren't you?"

"You remind me of my brother." Jake raked a hand through his hair in frustration. "Andy can read minds, too. Do they teach you how to do that in the seminary?"

"I like your brother already."

"Everyone does." Jake could say it without a twinge of envy. "It's too bad you got stuck with me instead of him." He was only half joking.

Matt chuckled. "I'm pretty sure God didn't look

down from Heaven and say, 'Pops, I sent the wrong brother to Mirror Lake.'"

Sometimes, Jake wasn't so sure.

"Before we get started, would everyone please join me in a word of prayer?"

Conversation around the table subsided as Pastor Wilde stepped to the front of the group. His easy smile swept over the people gathered together under the shade of the willow trees.

Emma bowed her head but didn't close her eyes, choosing to focus on a maple leaf near her foot. Scarlet trimmed the delicate edges, a sure sign that autumn was on its way.

She blocked out the pastor's words until she heard Abby, who was sitting across from her, echo his heartfelt amen. Emma lifted her head, ready to count the minutes until the meeting ended.

Harold Davis stepped forward and briefly shared the vision of the ministry and then Pastor Wilde introduced each of the mentors. Emma recognized some of the men from church and a few others from town. Each one took a few minutes to explain why he was involved in the ministry and then went on to share some of his hobbies and interests. After that, the pastor encouraged the mothers to ask questions and express any concerns they had about the program.

Most of them were excited about their sons having a male role model, but Emma couldn't lay aside the doubts that swept through her mind. Jeremy wasn't rowdy or rebellious. Not a "handful"; the word she'd heard some of the mothers use to describe their sons. When he showed an interest in something, she encouraged him to check out a book or do an Internet search on the topic.

Jeremy wasn't lacking anything. Was he? As her mother, it was her job to protect him. He had already experienced the loss of his father. Was it wrong of her to want to shield him from situations—or people—that could hurt him?

A sudden commotion interrupted the meeting as the boys spilled out of the woods. Abby's fiancé, Quinn O'Halloran, had taken them on a nature walk to keep them occupied during the question-and-answer session.

"I think that's our signal to adjourn." Pastor Matt smiled. "But please, feel free to stay as long as you like. We've organized a fishing tournament for the boys and thanks to Abby, there is still plenty of food left."

"Oops, that's my cue." Abby leaned over and gave Emma a quick hug, surrounding her with the faint but distinctive scent of cinnamon. "I'll call you about that business card."

"I better help her get ready for the second

wave." Kate stood up and pointed her plastic fork at Emma. "Stop by the café sometime." She lowered her voice. "People say that my pie is as good as Abby's."

"I heard that!" Abby called over her shoulder.

"You were supposed to." Kate rolled her eyes and aimed a smile at Emma, who couldn't muster one in return.

She'd been watching for Jeremy and her heart wrenched when she spotted him trailing behind the rest of the group, his hands clenched into fists at his sides.

This was what she'd been afraid would happen.

Chapter Six

Tamping down her concern, Emma waved to get Jeremy's attention. He saw her and ran over to the table.

"Is everything all right?"

"Look what I found!" Jeremy slid onto the bench next to her, his expression animated rather than upset. "Mr. O'Halloran said it's a real arrowhead. I found it when we were looking for deer antlers in the woods."

Emma looked down at the flat oval stone cradled in her son's grimy palm. The tiny notches on either side had definitely been put there by design, not accident.

"You don't stumble on one of these very often." An elderly man, whose dusky skin and coffee-brown eyes reflected his Native American ancestry, had walked over to examine the arrowhead. "Your son is quite the adventurer."

Jeremy's eyes glowed at the praise. "Just like we learned at camp. Right Mr. Redstone?"

"I'm glad you remembered." The man winked at him. "How are you doing with the rest of your explorations these days?"

"Good."

Daniel Redstone must have sensed Emma's confusion, because he turned back to Emma with a smile. "I volunteered with The Great Adventure Camp last month and Jeremy joined my group. All the boys committed to memorizing one scripture verse a week."

Emma felt the same way she had after admitting to Abby that Jeremy didn't know how to swim. He had tried to tell her about the things he'd learned at the church-sponsored day camp but Emma knew she'd been less than receptive. As sensitive as Jeremy was, he must have picked up on her feelings. As the week progressed, he'd talked less and less about the things they'd done on that particular day. At the time, she'd been relieved. Now she was simply embarrassed.

"I don't understand some of them," Jeremy admitted. "The words are kind of hard to read in Mom's Bible."

Mom's Bible?

Emma swallowed hard. She didn't own a Bible…

Yes, she did.

A palm-size edition, with print so small a person practically needed a magnifying glass to read it, bound in white leather. The clerk at the bridal store had given it to Emma when she'd purchased her gown. She vaguely remembered the woman smiling and telling her that it was the most important "accessory" a bride could have. After the wedding ceremony, Emma had carefully written Brian's name and her own in the front cover and recorded the date.

The beginning of their life together.

Emma hadn't seen the Bible for a long time. But somehow, Jeremy must have found it.

She pushed to her feet, overwhelmed by a sudden urge to escape. "We have to go."

"But Mom!" Jeremy's voice rose in dismay. "There's going to be a fishing tournament. Can't we stay a little longer?"

"We agreed to attend the picnic," Emma said, careful not to look at Jeremy and see the disappointment in his eyes. "And the picnic is over."

She'd kept her part of the deal. Now Jeremy would have to accept her decision.

"Chief Sutton! Why do I get the impression that you aren't taking me seriously?"

Jake held the phone a few inches away from

his ear but it didn't muffle Delia Peake's piercing soprano. Her voice sounded pleasant enough when it blended with the rest of the church choir but not when she was using it to drill a hole in his eardrum.

"I suppose I could take an impression of the foot—*paw*—print, Mrs. Peake, but it would be difficult to match it to a specific suspect…" Jake closed his eyes. "No, I must have missed that episode, but no matter what you saw on television, I don't think it's possible to trace the damage done to your garden to a *particular* raccoon."

A rap on the door brought Jake's head up. His prayer for deliverance had been answered.

Thank you, Lord.

"Mrs. Peake? I'm sorry, but my nine-o'clock appointment is here." Jake didn't know who that nine o'clock appointment was, but it didn't matter. He was grateful for their arrival as he hung up the phone.

The door opened and Matt Wilde sauntered in.

Or not.

"TowhatdoIowethisunexpectedvisit?" As relieved as Jake was at the interruption, an internal alarm went off at the sight of the serious expression on the pastor's face.

"I have a problem."

Jake's eyes narrowed as he leaned back in the chair. "Why do I get the feeling that your problem is about to become my problem?"

"I think you should rethink your decision to become a mentor."

"Matt—"

"Just hear me out. Please."

"Fine," Jake said irritably. "But only because you used the magic word."

Matt, like Andy, seemed to have a Teflon coating when it came to sarcasm. He dropped into the chair opposite Jake's desk instead of running for cover.

"We had a lot more boys show up yesterday than we anticipated, praise God."

Jake couldn't argue with that. It *was* a praise. New as he was to a life of faith, answered prayer still blew him away. But that didn't mean he trusted the look in Matt's eyes.

"I did volunteer for the prayer team, remember?"

"You can be on the prayer team."

"Good—"

"*And* serve as a mentor."

"What makes you so sure I can do this?" Jake's hands fisted on the desk.

"What makes you sure you can't?" Matt countered mildly.

Because I'm not sure I have anything valuable to offer, Jake wanted to say. How could he be a good influence on a person when he hadn't noticed his best friend drifting closer to the line between right and wrong? But he wasn't ready to share that story. Not even with Matt. The physical wounds he'd suffered had healed faster than the emotional ones.

"I have no idea how to relate to kids." Frustration leeched into his voice. "If God wants me to be involved in something, shouldn't it at least be something I'm *good* at?"

Something that didn't make him feel totally inadequate?

"You must be better than you think." Matt leaned back and crossed his hands behind his head. "One of the boys specifically requested you."

"Requested me?" Jake couldn't believe it. He hadn't mingled with the boys at the picnic the day before. He hadn't joined in the games with the pastor and Quinn O'Halloran. In fact, the only boy he'd had any interaction with at all had been...

Jake's head jerked up and he met Matt's amused gaze.

"That's right. Jeremy Barlow."

The name brought Jake to his feet. "Are you saying that Emma agreed to let Jeremy participate?"

"Not yet."

"You'll never be able to convince her."

"You're probably right." Matt's smiled turned smug. "That's why I'm hoping you can."

I'll trust that You know what You're doing, God.

Jake muttered the prayer five minutes later as he crossed Main Street. Veering toward the one-story brick building on the corner, he followed the cobblestone walkway to the door and paused to read the bronze plaque before going inside.

The building had once housed the first one-room schoolhouse in the county. Vacant for years, it had been saved from being turned into a parking lot by a group of citizens who later formed the local historical society.

The details were printed in letters so small that Jake had to squint to read them. But he did—because knowing local history was important.

Not because he was stalling.

And not because he was sure that he was the last person Emma expected—or wanted—to walk into the library.

Jake slipped inside the building, careful not to let the door slam shut behind him. It was the first time he'd been inside the library. Sunlight poured through the lace curtains, creating stencils on the gleaming hardwood floor. Bookshelves fanned out like the spokes of a wheel from the massive circular oak desk in the center of the room. The air smelled like lemon polish.

The order and tidiness reminded him of a certain librarian.

Jake looked around. There was no sign of Emma.

He was about to ring the bell when he heard a voice coming from the back of the room. Jake followed the sound through the maze of tables and suddenly felt as if he'd fallen through a rabbit hole. Everything around him suddenly shrank in size. The tables and chairs. The bookshelves.

Behind a portable room divider, painted in bright colors and cut out to resemble a storybook forest scene, he heard a soft giggle.

"'Watch what I do! I'll bake cookies and bread. Yummy pies, tarts and cakes,' Chef Charlotte said…"

The lilting voice sounded vaguely familiar.

Jake moved closer and peeked through a narrow gap in the divider.

A dozen children sat in a semicircle on a colorful rag rug. All eyes were riveted on the woman who sat cross-legged in front of them, holding a picture book on her lap. A snow-white apron shrouded her slim frame and a tall chef's hat was propped on the tawny head, but there was no mistaking the face that had been invading his thoughts. Even with the tip of her nose and porcelain cheeks dusted with something that looked like…flour.

The children, who had obviously heard the story before, all shouted together on cue. "What will you do with your cakes and bread?"

"'I'll give them away,' Chef Charlotte said." With a flourish, Emma waved a wooden spoon in the air as if it were a scepter.

Jake could feel his chin scraping against the floor.

What had happened to the Emma Barlow he knew? The buttoned-up woman who had worn a skirt and blouse to a Saturday picnic? The one who didn't seem to *like* people?

Or maybe, Jake had a sudden epiphany, it was just him that she didn't like.

"Who's that?"

Jake stepped back but not fast enough. The freckle-faced boy who'd spotted him pointed to the gap in the divider, giving away Jake's exact location.

"It's a stranger!" The little girl sitting closest to Emma let out a shriek with a decibel level high enough to break glass.

"Stranger, stranger!" The rest took up the chant.

Jake winced.

"No, it's not." One brave little soul had peered around the divider. "It's a p'liceman. He gotsa badge, see?"

Before Jake could blink, a pint-size posse surrounded him. He was, to use official police jargon, *busted*.

"Are you going to read us a story like Miss Emma?" A petite girl with melting dark eyes and a cloud of black curls tugged on his pant leg.

Jake shot Emma a panicked look.

"That's a good idea, Hannah." Emma's smile made Jake's blood run cold. "And I think I know the perfect one for Chief Sutton, don't you?"

"Sheriff Ben Rides Again!" The children hopped up and down, making Jake feel as if he were caught in a blender. They captured him before he could protest, towing him over to the rag rug Emma had occupied moments ago. Jake felt a little like Gulliver amid the Lilliputians.

Emma managed to work her way to the front of the jubilant crowd. Relieved, Jake smiled. But instead of rescuing him, she handed him an over-size picture book. And a stick horse with a tangled mane of red yarn and button eyes.

Jake couldn't believe she hadn't put a stop to this yet. She should be upset that he'd interrupted her story time…

Their eyes met over the children's heads and Jake suddenly understood.

This was a challenge.

And Jake never—*never*—walked away from a challenge. He unleashed a slow smile in Emma's direction.

"Don't *I* get a hat?"

Hat.

Emma suddenly remembered the chef's hat perched on her head. She swept it off and smoothed away some flyaway strands of hair from her face.

The bells over the door of the library usually alerted her if a patron entered the library, but the story she'd been reading was interactive and this particular group of five- and six-year-olds tended to be a bit exuberant.

As Jake would soon discover.

Emma almost felt sorry for him. Almost.

The man *should* be shaking in his boots for sneaking up on her like that.

How long had he been watching her? And why?

She had the uneasy feeling it wasn't because he needed a library card. And if he did, Emma doubted that he would stop in while on duty. Did his visit have something to do with the stolen property that Jeremy had found on Saturday?

The thought should have made her relax, but it didn't. If she was uncomfortable, Emma deemed it only fair that Jake Sutton be uncomfortable, as well.

Except that Jake didn't appear uncomfortable at all.

Reggie, the boy who'd spotted Jake hiding behind the divider, retrieved a battered cowboy hat from the trunk of dress-up clothes and handed it to him. Jake tapped it against his thigh a few times, almost as if he were pretending to dislodge some invisible trail dust clinging to it.

"I can't see, Ms. Emma!" Hannah tugged on the hem of her apron.

Emma scooted to the side. She didn't even have to remind the children to take a seat. They dropped like stones onto the rug when Jake lightly cleared his throat. He opened the book and thumbed to the first page.

"Sheriff Ben was getting old. Too old to keep the peace in a town like Cutter Bend," Jake read. "His bones were tired and creaky and he got sore when he rode his mule into town…" He paused and shot her a suspicious look. "Local law enforcement rides a *mule?*"

"Gracie!" one of the girls squealed.

"A mule," Jake muttered. "Named Gracie."

"Read it! Read it!" The words became a chant, coupled with a rhythmic pounding of little hands against the floor.

Emma nodded, pressing her lips together to seal in the smile she felt coming on. Any moment, Jake Sutton would find an excuse to flee like Snakebite Sam, Sheriff Ben's archenemy…

Instead, he flicked the brim of the cowboy hat and it settled on his dark head at a jaunty angle.

The crushed black felt had never looked so attractive.

Emma swallowed hard, her fist clenching the wooden spoon she still held in her hand. The fluttery feeling that started in her knees and worked its way to her heart whenever Jake Sutton came into view was unexpected. Unnerving. And totally unacceptable.

But acknowledging that didn't make it go away.

"Sheriff Ben had achy bones and his eyesight wasn't as good as it used to be, but he wasn't afraid of anyone. Not even—" Jake paused dramatically and all the children leaned forward in a hushed silence, eyes wide as they waited for him to continue even though they'd heard the story a dozen times "—Snakebite Sam."

Chapter Seven

As the last of the children danced out the door, Emma took refuge behind the desk, putting something solid between her and Jake.

She thought he would leave when he realized how busy she was. But no. Jake had joined the story-time group for snack time. He'd lowered his lean frame onto one of the tiny wooden chairs and accepted a pink frosted cupcake in honor of Hannah Cohen's fifth birthday. He had sipped pretend tea from a pink teacup and politely declined the use of the lavender feather boa one of the girls offered to drape around his neck.

Emma would have thought the *sight* of a feather boa would have sent Jake running for the door.

But here he was. Prowling around her desk. Forcing Emma to turn a complete circle while she kept a wary eye on him.

"This is a nice library."

"Thank you."

"How long have you worked here?"

Emma moistened her lips. "Six years."

The answer hung in the air between them.

"I see," Jake said after a moment.

Did he, Emma wondered with a trace of bitterness. She glanced at the door, hoping someone—anyone—would come into the library and give her an excuse to escape. But now that the children had gone home, the noon hour tended to be slow. School would be starting in a few weeks and the last days of balmy temperatures would soon be a memory. People wanted to soak up the last bit of sunshine rather than check out a book to read.

Emma decided she had no option but to face his unexpected presence head-on.

"What can I do for you, Chief Sutton?"

"You can start by calling me Jake, remember?"

Emma wanted to say that wasn't a good idea, only she wasn't sure why. In a town the size of Mirror Lake, no one stood on ceremony. She'd even heard several people call Pastor Wilde by his first name at the picnic. But how could she explain to Jake that dropping his title felt as if she were removing a barrier?

A barrier Emma didn't *want* removed.

"Is this about the tools that Jeremy found? Does

he have to make some kind of statement?" She hoped not. If Jeremy had to give a formal statement, it would mean a trip to the police department, and Emma had no desire to go there ever again. Just the thought tied her stomach into knots.

"No, this isn't about the tools—"

"Then if you'd like a library card, you can fill out this form." Emma gestured toward the applications stacked neatly in a plastic tray. "And I will need to see proof of residence."

"I stopped by to talk to you about the mentoring ministry that Church of the Pines started."

Emma's mouth turned as dry as the chalk she'd dusted on her cheeks before reading *Charlotte the Chef.* "I didn't realize you were involved."

"I'm on the prayer team." Jake's lips twisted in a wry smile. "But I also told the pastor I'd be willing to do whatever God wants me to."

Did he think that meant trying to change her mind?

"I planned to call Pastor Wilde today and let him know that Jeremy won't be able to participate." Although, knowing how disappointed he would be, Emma hadn't broken the news to her son.

"He wants to be involved, Emma."

Emma's heart gave a little kick when Jake said her name.

"He also wants to eat hot dogs for breakfast." She managed to lift her chin and meet that unsettling amber gaze straight on. "That doesn't mean it's good for him."

This was going to be more difficult than he thought.

Emma had scrambled for cover behind the desk the moment they were alone. Jake didn't know why she'd bothered. The rigid set of her shoulders and the wary look in her eyes proved effective enough barriers.

To anyone but him.

He might have been tempted to give up and walk out the door if the conversation he'd had with Matt wasn't still lodged in his head.

"Jeremy Barlow called the church an hour ago," Matt had told him. "That kid is something else. He said he's been praying about it and he is convinced that *you* are supposed to be his mentor."

"Did he say why?"

"No." Matt's smile had faded. "But it could have something to do with his dad being a police officer. It would make sense, wouldn't it? A boy that age might be curious about a man who pursued the same career as his father."

A career that had taken that father's life.

Jake had released a slow breath. There was a strong possibility that the reason Jeremy had chosen him as a mentor would be the same reason Emma would reject him.

She looked tempted to show him the door now. Fortunately, the library was open to the public so she had to endure his presence for the moment.

Okay, Lord, if this is Your idea, You are going to have to give me some wisdom here. I have no idea how to change Emma's mind.

Although it suddenly became clear to Jake that he wanted to.

What had started out as curiosity had undergone a subtle shift over the past hour. Maybe it had something to do with the fact that he'd seen Emma with her defenses down, waving a rolling pin as she recited a story for a mesmerized group of kindergartners.

To be honest, Jake had been a little mesmerized himself by the undercurrent of laughter he'd heard in her voice. The dusting of flour on the tip of Emma's nose that elevated her already pretty features to a winsome beauty.

She met his gaze, shields once again in place, but this time Jake looked past the stubborn tilt of her chin and saw the vulnerable curve of her lips, and the fear crouched behind the defiant look in her eyes.

With a flash of insight that Jake assumed was an answer to his prayer, he heard himself ask, "How old was Jeremy when Brian died?"

The color drained from Emma's face and she flinched, leaving Jake to wonder how long it had been since she'd heard anyone say her husband's name.

Forget the barrier she'd put between them. In two strides, Jake was standing next to her. Not close enough to crowd, but close enough to catch her if she passed out on him.

Emma folded her arms across her chest. For a second, Jake didn't think she was going to answer. When she did, the word came out in a whisper.

"Four."

Jake had suspected Jeremy must have been close to that age when he'd lost his father, but hearing Emma confirm it twisted his gut.

What now, Lord?

In his former line of work, Jake had extracted information from people with the precision of a surgeon but now things had changed. *He* had changed. Jake knew he couldn't stir the well of Emma's grief and find the answers he was seeking without God's help.

"Does Jeremy ask a lot of questions about him?"

he asked, feeling his way through unfamiliar territory.

"No." Emma hesitated. "He used to."

Jake read between the lines. Jeremy had asked questions until he was old enough to realize that it hurt his mother to talk about it.

"You're doing a great job with him, Emma," he said. "Jeremy is bright. Curious. To tell you the truth, I'm a little intimidated by a kid who put down the word research under his list of hobbies and interests."

A ghost of a smile lifted the corners of her lips. "I've always encouraged him to study. To seek out the answers to his questions."

"That's what I mean." Jake was stunned by a sudden longing to see the rest of that smile. "I think Jeremy is at the age where he wants to test himself. Boys want to know what they're made of. Push the limits a little. And you want him to do that." He saw panic flare in Emma's eyes and added swiftly, "In healthy ways. Ways that will help him make a smooth transition from boy to man."

Emma remained silent.

"Emma?"

She looked at him and Jake could see the battle being played out in those expressive blue eyes.

"What are you afraid of?"

* * *

What was she afraid of?

There were so many things to choose from, Emma wasn't sure she could pick out only one.

She was afraid that letting Jeremy spend time with a mentor would prove that she wasn't doing her job.

She was afraid her son would need her less…or not at all.

She was afraid of letting Jeremy out of her sight because he was the only family she had left.

And she was afraid of the disturbing feelings that Jake Sutton stirred inside of her. Feelings Emma thought had been buried along with Brian.

He was close. Too close. Whenever Emma drew in a breath, the clean scent of Jake's soap, mingled with a hint of lime, came with it, muddling her senses.

"I appreciate what Pastor Wilde is trying to do," Emma said stiffly. "I'm sure there are boys who would benefit from the mentoring program. But to be perfectly honest, I can't imagine allowing Jeremy to spend time with a stranger."

"What if the person wasn't a stranger? Would that make a difference?"

"I don't know." Emma tucked her lower lip between her teeth as she considered the question. "I suppose it might. But we haven't been going to church very long. Jeremy doesn't know many people."

And neither did she. Living in a small town, where it seemed as if everyone knew each other, had been intimidating to a young woman who had never settled in one place for very long. Emma had been more than content to remain in the background. After Brian's death, she had retreated even further in an attempt to avoid the awkward silences and the pity she saw on people's faces.

"He knows me," Jake said.

"You?" Emma almost choked on the word.

Jake didn't look offended by her strong reaction. "He called Pastor Matt this morning and requested that I be his mentor."

Requested. Jake Sutton.

Oh, Jeremy.

"But..." Emma pressed one hand against her forehead, trying to sort through this latest complication. "I don't understand."

But then again, maybe she did.

On her way to bed the night before, Emma had noticed a sliver of light under Jeremy's bedroom door. That hadn't surprised her. More often than not, she would find her son sound asleep with a book still propped up in his lap.

Only he hadn't been asleep. He'd been sitting

up in bed, his gaze fixed on the arrowhead in his hand.

"And here I thought I'd find you reading up on Native American artifacts," Emma had gently teased.

"It's not the same." Jeremy had run his thumb over the jagged edges of the stone. The sparkle in his eyes had warned Emma that a change was coming. A change she didn't understand but knew she couldn't prevent.

He wanted to *find* arrowheads, not read about them.

That simple statement forced Emma to face her own limitations. Forced her to acknowledge that Jeremy needed something that she couldn't give him. She remembered the way Jake had boosted his confidence by letting him dig the hole for the apple tree.

How had Jake put it? That boys needed to test themselves?

The thought both terrified Emma and made her proud of her son at the same time.

But Jake Sutton?

A man who, like Brian, had chosen a dangerous career. A man whose scarred jaw and measured gaze were an unsettling contradiction to the one who'd clapped a battered cowboy hat on his head and completely charmed a rambunctious group of children.

If he saw Jeremy on a regular basis, did that mean she would have to see *him?*

Emma's knees turned to liquid at the thought.

"Would you consider letting Jeremy and me spend some time together for a trial period?" Jake asked. "After that, if you still believe it's a bad idea, you can withdraw him from the program. If you explained it to Jeremy, I think he would agree to that."

So did Emma. After all, as her son was quick to point out these days, it was *reasonable* for a person to check things out before they made a decision. If only she'd known her favorite saying would be used against her!

"A trial period," she repeated.

"How about a month?"

"I don't know." *I don't know you.* "What are your qualifications? Have you been involved in a mentoring program before?"

Jake looked up at the ceiling, providing Emma with a closer view of the pale grid of scars etching his jaw. "I don't have any experience with kids. This is all new to me, too."

It was the last thing Emma had expected him to admit.

"Then give me one good reason why I should trust you with my son."

"Because Jeremy wants you to."

Now who wasn't playing fair? Emma thought. Jake had to know that Jeremy was her reason for getting up in the morning. The last thing she wanted to do was deny her son something that put a sparkle in his eyes. Like the one she'd seen when he'd shown her the arrowhead...and talked about the crime that he and Jake had "solved together" on Saturday.

"Why do *you* want to do this?" Emma asked.

Jake's lips quirked. "Because Jeremy wants me to."

The same reason. Like it or not, concern for her son had become a connecting point between them.

"I'll agree to a month." Emma hoped she wasn't making a huge mistake.

"I'll tell Pastor Wilde." Jake started to walk away but paused when he reached the door. "And Emma?"

She forced herself to look at him.

"You *can* trust me."

As soon as the door closed, Emma sank against the desk.

Trust him?

At the moment, it was the feelings Jake stirred up inside of her that she didn't trust.

Chapter Eight

Jake's cell phone rang less than five minutes after he walked into the house.

He glanced at the tiny screen to read the name before answering it. It seemed that someone—and Jake had a hunch that someone's name was Delia Peake—had given his private number to everyone in Mirror Lake.

This time, however, it was safe to pick up.

"Whatsup, Bro?" Andy's cheerful greeting came over the line.

"Whatsup, *Bro?*" Jake echoed. "You've been spending too much time with the kids in your youth group."

But even as he gave Andy a hard time, Jake was glad the term "brother" came so easily. Jake had been twelve, Andy three years younger, when Jake's mom and Andy's dad had fallen in love. They had become linked together by their parents' marriage certificate, not blood. Jake and his best friend, Sean, had tormented the poor kid every chance they got, but Andy had never complained or tried to get back at him. Jake had thought of Sean as his brother, but when push came to shove, it had been Andy who hadn't given up on him. It was his prayers that had pulled Jake out of the darkness.

"There's no such thing as too much time with my kids," Andy said loyally. The thing was, Jake knew he meant it. "Are you on duty or off?"

"Am I ever off duty?"

"Should I get out my violin?" Andy paused. "Or my harp?"

"Did you call just to harass me?" Jake laughed, the sound of his brother's voice easing some of the tension that had settled in his shoulders after his visit to the library that morning.

"As entertaining as that can be, I called because God brought your name up while I was praying today."

"What time was that?" Jake asked suspiciously.

"This morning. About eleven o'clock."

Eleven o'clock. Roughly the same time he had gone to see Emma at the library.

Was he being tag-teamed?

"Really?"

"Yes, really. So, are you going to tell me why?"

Jake knew he could sum it up in two words. Emma Barlow. But he wasn't sure what would happen if he trusted that kind of intel to his kid brother.

That Emma had agreed—albeit reluctantly—to let him spend time with Jeremy on a trial basis had been nothing less than a miracle. Jake hadn't been quite sure how he'd come up with the idea...until now.

"Probably because I needed an extra dose of courage," Jake admitted.

"You?" Now it was Andy's turn to laugh. "The undercover drug officer? The guy who walked into crack houses without a weapon? Made deals with the thugs whose pictures are on the bulletin board at the post office?"

Compared to Jake's newest assignment, his previous job *still* looked easier.

"The church I've been attending started a mentoring ministry. I got drafted."

And even more specifically, *requested*. In spite of his misgivings, that had been the reason Jake hadn't been able to say no.

That and two matching pairs of wide, gray-blue eyes.

"You? You're going to be a mentor to a...kid?"

"That's usually who needs a mentor. Are you laughing?" Jake demanded.

"No…" A series of muffled snorts followed the word.

"Uh-huh." Jake didn't have to be in the same room as his brother to know he was rolling on the floor. "I tried to tell the pastor it was a bad idea."

"What are you talking about?" Andy sobered immediately. "It's a great idea."

"You of all people should know that isn't true. Some people could question my judgment. My ability to be a good influence."

On the other side of the line, Andy expelled a slow breath. "You have to let it go, Jake," he said quietly. "No one saw the signs."

That wasn't much of a consolation. "I should have seen it. Sean was my best friend."

That was the thing about dwelling in the shadows for so long. Eventually, they began to blur a person's perspective. Wrong started to look like… right.

"Sean made his choice. And if he'd had his way, we wouldn't be having this conversation."

A shared memory weighted the silence that fell between them. Andy's stricken face staring down at Jake when the paramedics wheeled him into the

E.R. Both of them unsure if they'd ever see each other again.

As often as Jake had brushed aside Andy's faith or, even worse, poked fun at his brother for dropping out of medical school to attend the seminary instead, he hadn't felt as if he could appeal to God for help the night of the drug bust. The only thing Jake could do was look into the cold eye of the gun pointed at him and apologize to God for being stubborn. Tell Him that he wished he would have taken time to know Him when he'd had the chance—that he would do things differently if he could.

God hadn't only heard his prayer, He had intervened in a way that left Jake feeling a little like the apostle Paul on the road to Damascus.

Because the second bullet—the one aimed at his forehead—never left the gun. It jammed. And then the man holding it had crumpled to the floor, two feet away from Jake, before he could try again.

In his head, Jake knew what Andy said about Sean was right. It was taking his heart a little longer to catch up.

He rose to his feet and took a restless lap around the room. "For now, it looks like God wants me to spend some time with Jeremy, but I could definitely use some pointers."

"You're asking me for advice?" Andy's tone

lightened, as if he sensed Jake's reluctance to talk about Sean.

"Don't let it go to your head. Kids are your thing, not mine."

"When do they match you up with someone?"

"They already did."

Andy's low whistle made Jake smile. "I told you that God wasn't going to waste any time. What's his name?"

"Jeremy Barlow."

"Troublemaker?"

"Not even close. Jeremy is on the shy side. Doesn't seem to have many friends. He's definitely a thinker."

"Rough home life?"

Rough home life.

Jake turned the words over. In his mind's eye, he could see an older house and the front porch that begged for a coat of paint. The twenty-year shingles on the roof that looked as if they'd been forced to last thirty. All home-maintenance projects that would have fallen on Brian Barlow's shoulders and yet they'd become another burden for Emma to bear.

He had no doubt the citizens of Mirror Lake would have chipped in to help if Emma had only let people know she had a need. He had a hunch that something beyond grief added to her resistance. No one could find fault, however, with her parenting.

"Emma is doing a good job but she can't do everything."

"Whoa, hold on a second," Andy said. "No need to get defensive. It was a question, not a judgment. And who is Emma?"

"Jeremy's mom. Her husband was a cop here in Mirror Lake. He died six years ago in a high-speed chase. Jeremy was only four years old at the time."

"That's rough. So how does she feel about you mentoring Jeremy?"

"She doesn't…approve of me."

"But you're one of the good guys," Andy protested.

"I'm not sure she thinks so," Jake said. "She's very protective. And she isn't sold on the idea of her son spending time with someone she doesn't know."

"I have the perfect solution for that."

"You do?"

"Let her get to know you."

"Jake wants to take me fishing, Mom!"

Emma's heart turned a somersault at the announcement. The fact that she knew this was coming, had even agreed to it, didn't seem to matter when faced with the reality of what she'd agreed to.

For Jeremy's sake, Emma tried not to let him see her reaction. "When?"

"Tomorrow night." Jeremy's thin frame practically vibrated with excitement. "But he said to make sure it was okay with you first."

How nice of Jake, Emma thought. She didn't want him to be thoughtful. Or considerate. It was easier to keep her distance when all she saw was a badge.

Jake had claimed he understood how difficult it was for her to let Jeremy spend time with him, and yet their very first outing was a fishing trip. Couldn't he have chosen something that didn't involve water? What was wrong with going out for ice cream? Playing catch at the ball field? Not that Jeremy *liked* baseball, but still…

"You don't have a fishing pole." A weak excuse, but the only one she could come up with on such short notice.

"I saw one in the shed."

Emma turned toward the sink, blinking back the tears that blurred her vision. After Brian's death, other than a few special mementos she'd saved for Jeremy, Emma had given the rest of his things to a local charity. She didn't remember keeping his fishing pole.

"So, can I go?" Jeremy pleaded.

"I suppose."

He let out a whoop that rattled the light fixture on the ceiling. "Really? You won't be mad?"

The innocent question pierced Emma's conscience.

Had she really been that unreasonable lately?

Yes, she had.

Emma forced a smile. "I won't be mad."

Jeremy lifted the telephone that Emma hadn't seen clutched in his hand. "Mom says it's okay."

Jake was on the phone? Emma hadn't even heard it ring! She stifled a groan. Had he heard her pitiful attempt to discourage her son from going?

Probably.

"Okay." Jeremy's smile didn't dim. "Here she is." He handed her the phone. "Jake wants to talk to you."

"H-hello."

"Hi, Emma." Jake's husky voice raised goose bumps on her arms. "If I didn't have a city council meeting tomorrow after work, I would accept your dinner invitation."

Her *dinner* invitation?

"I...understand." Emma understood that she and her son were going to sit down and have a talk!

"I'll definitely take you up on it another time, though."

"Another time," she echoed faintly.

"I'll stop by around six o'clock to pick up Jeremy, if that works for you."

"He's looking forward to it."

"So am I."

Emma hung up the phone and turned on her son. "Jeremy Barlow—don't you ever invite someone to dinner without asking me first."

The guileless blue eyes widened. "But Mom, don't you like Jake?"

The unexpected question punched the air from Emma's lungs. "It doesn't matter if I like him."

"Yes, it does." Jeremy's worried expression heaped guilt on top of her anxiety.

"I like him." Emma pushed the words out. "He seems…nice." Inwardly she winced at the generic description. One that didn't begin to describe the man whose unexpected appearance at the library the day before had turned her world upside down.

The answer seemed to satisfy Jeremy, however, because his sunny smile returned. "I like him, too. A lot."

That was another thing Emma was afraid of.

Jake turned off the ignition and stared at Emma's house, wondering how he could convince her to let him tackle some of the minor repairs around the place. It had been difficult enough to get her to agree to let him spend time with Jeremy.

Window boxes filled with yellow flowers and rose bushes planted along the stone foundation added homey touches but couldn't hide the peeling paint or the porch that listed to one side.

As he got out of the car, the front door flew open.

"Hi, Jake!" Jeremy hurtled toward him.

"Ready to do some fishing?"

"Yup." Jeremy nodded vigorously. "I found a pole in the shed. It was my dad's."

The announcement stripped the air from Jake's lungs. He wanted to be there for Jeremy, but what if his efforts only succeeded in bringing back painful memories for Emma?

Then you'll be out of their lives in a month, he reminded himself.

For some reason, the thought settled like a weight on Jake's chest. What was the matter with him? He didn't form attachments easily and yet somehow, Emma and her son had already worked their way under his skin.

"The trunk is open. Go ahead and load up your stuff," Jake instructed. "I have to talk to your mom."

"Okay." Jeremy headed for the car. "She's inside."

Jake rapped on the door but didn't wait for an invitation before going inside. Emma might have had trouble keeping up with general maintenance on the outside of the house, but on the inside, pale yellow walls and white crown molding gave the interior a warm, welcoming look.

The foyer branched off in several directions so Jake picked the one that he guessed would lead him to the kitchen.

His heart tipped at the sight of Emma standing in the middle of the room, hands propped on her slender hips as she stared down at an enormous wicker trunk. Tendrils of honey-streaked hair had escaped the wide gold clip at the nape of her neck and framed her delicate features.

Jake fought a sudden urge to smooth them back into place.

He'd deliberately scheduled some time with Jeremy right away—before Emma could change her mind—but the pensive expression on her face pinched his conscience. It was clear that even though Emma had approved the fishing trip, she was having second thoughts about letting her son go.

He braced a hand on each side of the doorway. "I did knock."

Emma visibly started at the sound of his voice. "Jake."

Finally. Jake had started to wonder if she would ever drop the title and call him by his first name. He nodded at the trunk. "Do you need some help with that?"

"Thank you." Emma's polite mask fell back into place. "It is a little heavy."

"Where does it go?"

"Wherever you have room."

Wherever *he* had room?

"You want me to take this along?" Jake had to be sure he understood.

Emma nodded. "I packed a few things in the picnic basket for you and Jeremy."

A picnic basket? It was closer to the size of a laundry hamper.

Jake clamped down on a smile. Even with his rusty social skills, he knew it probably wouldn't be a good idea to point out they were only going to be gone a few hours. "What's in it?"

"Juice boxes. Oatmeal cookies."

"Healthy." Jake hoped that Jeremy would have room for an ice-cream sundae on the way home.

"Disposable washcloths."

"Always a good idea." When Jake saw Emma's frown, he decided it might be wiser to simply smile and nod.

"I don't have bug spray," Emma said. "Did you bring some?"

Jake had a hunch he was being tested. But fortunately, he knew the correct answer. Emma wasn't the only one who had come prepared.

"It's in the tackle box. Right next to the first-aid kit."

The flash of startled approval in Emma's eyes had Jake silently thanking the mother of twin boys who'd been standing behind him in line at the sporting-goods store. She'd overheard Jake talking to the cashier about his upcoming fishing trip and handed him the little white box.

"You'll need one of these," she'd whispered.

Jake had glanced at the red cross stamped on the cover—and then at the price tag. "Ten dollars for Band-Aids and antibiotic ointment?"

"Ten dollars for peace of mind," the woman had said with a wise smile.

Without another word, Jake had tossed it into the cart. Now he was glad he had.

Jeremy skidded into the kitchen. "I'm ready, Jake. Let's go!"

Chapter Nine

Emma laced her fingers together to stop them from shaking. She wished she could take back her decision. Wished that some things could stay the same.

But she forced a smile on the outside so her sensitive son wouldn't suspect that she was crumbling on the *inside*.

"Did you remember your jacket?"

"I have a sweatshirt. It's not cold out, Mom."

She caught her lip between her teeth. "I guess you're right."

"Why don't you get in the car, Jeremy?" Jake suggested softly. "I'll be right there."

"Okay." Jeremy ran over and locked his arms around her waist. "Bye, Mom!"

"Bye, sweetheart."

Jeremy squirmed in her arms and Emma forced

herself to let go. Now if only she could hold herself together a few more seconds until Jake left.

Only he didn't leave.

"Are you all right?"

"I'll be fine." When they returned.

"I remember when I was a kid, my mom always wanted to know one thing if I made plans to do something. *Details.*" Jake reached down and picked up the wicker basket. "Of course I didn't realize at the time that her 'one thing' really meant a lot of things. I thought I was getting off easy." He flashed the smile that never failed to set her pulse racing.

Emma wanted to return his smile. She stared at a point over his shoulder instead.

"Since Jeremy doesn't know what we're going to do this evening, I'll fill you in," Jake said, as if she'd asked. "We're not taking a boat out on the lake. Abby offered the use of her dock at the lodge. I'll make sure Jeremy wears a life jacket, since you mentioned that he doesn't know how to swim. I can though, by the way." He handed her a piece of paper. "Here's my cell phone number. Feel free to call. Just to say hello, if you want to."

Jake had read her mind.

Emma didn't know whether to be relieved or terrified. And she could see that he wasn't poking fun at her concerns, he was trying to ease them.

Emma wasn't used to having someone who could read her thoughts so easily. Wasn't used to letting someone *close* enough to read her thoughts.

"Thank you." She focused on the number written on the piece of paper, silently willing him to go, but it was clear Jake wasn't finished with her yet.

"Now it's my turn to get some details from you. What time would you like me to bring Jeremy home?"

"How about eight o'clock?" Two hours should be more than enough time to catch a few fish, Emma reasoned.

"All right." Jake tilted his head. Studied her. And then, "Would you like to come with us?"

Emma didn't think she'd heard him right. "With you?"

"Sure. I don't mind and I'm sure Jeremy wouldn't, either."

Emma was tempted by the invitation. But the whole idea behind the mentoring program was to give Jeremy an opportunity to spend time with the mentor, not the mother.

"No, you two go ahead. Male bonding and all that." She ran damp palms down the front of her khaki skirt. "I have a project I'm working on for Abby."

"Are you sure?"

"I'm sure." She wasn't. Not at all. "I'll see you in a few hours."

"I'll take good care of him, Emma."

"I know you will."

Surprise flared in Jake's eyes but Emma couldn't blame him.

She'd surprised herself.

"When can we go fishing again, Jake?"

"I'm not sure." It was the second time Jeremy had asked the question since they'd left Mirror Lake Lodge, and now that his house was in sight, he was eager for an answer.

The porch light flickered a welcome as Jake parked the car in the driveway. Had Emma spent the entire evening staring out the window, counting the minutes until they returned?

Jake had made a point to get Jeremy home early. He knew what it had cost Emma to turn down his invitation to go fishing with them. She could have gone along and kept an eye on her son, and yet she hadn't wanted to get in the way of "male bonding." The last thing Jake wanted to do was damage the fragile trust she'd placed in him.

"I'll have to check with your mom first."

"You can talk to her now." Jeremy unbuckled his seat belt and bailed out of the car, leaving behind the faint but unmistakable scent of fish in the air.

He may have brought Jeremy home early but not exactly in the same condition the boy had been in when they left.

Not that he was, either.

A ribbon of light unfurled across the yard as Emma opened the door and stepped onto the porch.

"Hi, Mom! We're back!"

"I see that." Emma's smile bloomed in response to her son's enthusiasm. "How was the fishing?"

"Great." Jeremy swaggered toward her, the fishing pole balanced on his shoulder. "We caught a lot, didn't we, Jake?"

"We did." They'd lost a lot more, but that had been his fault!

"Jake's going to cook them up for us next time."

If, Jake thought, there *was* a next time. Maybe Emma had changed her mind and decided that two hours, not four weeks, was enough of a "trial period."

A breeze stirred the evening air and Emma's nose wrinkled. "I think someone is going to need a shower before bed."

"Okay." Jeremy grinned and turned to Jake. "I had a lot of fun. Thanks, Jake." He ran into the house, leaving them alone with the awkward silence that fell between them.

Emma backed against the door. Judging from the uncertain look in her eyes, Jake guessed she was torn over whether or not to invite him in. He made the decision for her.

"I'll get the rest of the things out of the trunk, but before I do, this is for you." Jake held out a plastic cup.

"What is it?" Emma cast a dubious look at the contents.

"It's an ice-cream sundae. At least it used to be," Jake amended. The maraschino cherry that adorned the top had sunk to the bottom and the ice cream had changed from a solid to a liquid during the short drive from the Grapevine Café to the house. "Jeremy mentioned that hot fudge is your favorite kind."

"It is." Emma finally reached out and took the cup but she continued to stare down at the sundae as if she'd never seen one before.

"If it makes you feel better, we ate the oatmeal cookies first."

Emma smiled and Jake felt the impact down to his toes. It wasn't the first time he'd seen it, but it was the first time she'd directed it at *him*. It also gave him the courage to discover the answer to the question that had been chewing at the edge of his thoughts all evening.

"How did you do tonight?"

"It was…hard."

She'd told him the truth, so Jake decided he couldn't do any less.

"What would you say if I told you that I was just as afraid to take him as you were to let him go?"

Emma lifted curious eyes to his face. "What do you mean?"

Jake wasn't sure if he could even put it into words. Sitting on the dock, listening to Jeremy's laughter stir the evening air. Watching his expression when he reeled the first fish in. Seeing those blue eyes light up whenever Jake praised his effort.

It had left him feeling…renewed.

Until now, Jake hadn't realized the toll his undercover work had taken on him. The subtle change that occurred when a man grew so accustomed to the darkness that he forgot what it was like to live in the light.

Let Emma get to know you, Andy had said. But there were some things he couldn't tell her.

But he *could* tell her this.

Unable to resist this time, Jake reached out and tucked a strand of hair behind her ear. He leaned closer.

"I've never been fishing before."

Chapter Ten

Jake left Emma standing on the porch, trying to make sense of his words. And his touch.

Dazed, she made her way upstairs just as Jeremy emerged from the bathroom, his hair damp from the shower. With the dirt removed and a damp towel draped over his shoulder instead of a fishing creel, he looked more like her little boy. To Emma's relief, he smelled better, too.

"Did Jake leave?"

Emma managed a nod.

"Did you like the sundae?" Jeremy spotted the plastic cup in her hand. "It was Jake's idea."

"That was very thoughtful of him." She was beginning to see that's the kind of man Jake was. The kind who talked about his faith with the easy confidence of one who believed it. The kind who took a boy fishing and invited his mother along in order to ease her fears.

If only the others could be put to rest as easily, Emma thought.

Jeremy darted into his bedroom and flipped on the light on the nightstand. Emma followed, bending down to collect a trail of dirty clothes along the way.

"I'm glad you had a good time."

"You can come with us next time if you want to." Jeremy peeled back the comforter and dived beneath it.

"We'll see."

Emma decided to save that particular discussion for later. She reached for the light switch. "Do you want this off?"

"Not yet. I'm going to read awhile."

The librarian in Emma couldn't help but be pleased. "Let me guess—a book about fishing."

"Nope." Jeremy slid open the drawer in the nightstand and reached inside.

Emma sat down hard at the foot of the bed, her gaze riveted on the little white Bible Jeremy had tugged out of the drawer. "Where did you find that?"

"In a box of books downstairs." Jeremy looked surprised by the question. "Mr. Redstone told us that the Bible is one of the ways God talks to us, so I read it every night before I go to bed."

"I see." Emma moistened her lips, unsure of what to say. Or do.

A few days ago, she would have kissed Jeremy on the forehead and fled. Today, guilt weighed her down. She had always prided herself on having a close relationship with her son. Had always encouraged him to share his thoughts and ideas…until recently, since they'd started attending church.

Emma's conflicted emotions about faith clashed with the desire to understand her son's.

"What are you reading?"

Jeremy's shoulders relaxed and Emma knew she'd asked the right question. It hurt to realize that Jeremy hadn't thought he could share a part of his life that had become so important over the past few weeks.

"I'm reading the New Testament right now, but I told Jake that I'd look up his verse."

"*His* verse?" Emma said faintly.

Jeremy nodded. "He doesn't know many verses cause he's a new Christian, too, so he said he'd help me memorize mine if I helped him memorize his."

It didn't surprise Emma to discover that Jake was a Christian. He had volunteered with the mentoring ministry, after all. It was the "new" part that stirred her curiosity.

"Jake said his brother, Andy, told him to learn

this one." Jeremy thumbed through the translucent pages with a speed that made Emma blink. "Andy is a pastor, like Pastor Matt, only he talks to kids. He's the one who told Jake about God."

Emma's head started to spin. Apparently Jake and Jeremy had done more than fish that evening. Judging from the amount of information her son was sharing, they must have spent as much time, if not more, in conversation!

"Here it is. It's in Ephesians chapter three." Jeremy squinted at the tiny words. "Do you want me to read it out loud?"

Emma nodded, not trusting her voice at the moment.

"And I pray that you, being rooted and established in love, may have the power, together with all the saints, to grasp how wide and long and high and deep is the love of Christ." Jeremy read slowly, the tip of his finger tracing each word. "Wow, that's a long one," he said when he came to the end of the verse.

"Yes, it is." The room felt hot as the meaning of the words soaked in.

Why had Jake's brother chosen that particular passage of scripture? Did it hold some sort of special significance?

Why do you care? an inner voice chided.

Emma brushed the question away, afraid of what the answer might be.

"It's time for you to get some sleep now," she murmured.

"Are you going to pray with me tonight, too, Mom?"

Emma saw the expectant look on Jeremy's face and couldn't turn him down, even though it had been years since she had talked to God. But she wasn't willing to let her own doubts and insecurities sever the closeness between them.

"All right."

"I'll go first." Jeremy bowed his head. "God, thank You that Mom let me go fishing with Jake. Thanks for all the fish we caught and that it didn't rain. Help Jake memorize the long verse, because he said it gets harder to remember things when you get older…"

Emma found herself smiling, until Jeremy's elbow nudged her side. "It's your turn, Mom," he whispered.

"Sorry." She'd missed her cue.

As she opened her mouth, a wave of panic crashed over her.

Don't be silly, she thought, *just say something. Thank God for the sunshine…*

"You can tell Him anything, Mom," Jeremy whispered. "Mr. Redstone told us in Sunday school that you can be honest with God because nothing you say is going to change how much He loves you."

What about the things you *didn't* say, Emma thought. What if you'd stopped talking to God because you couldn't find the words that described how you were feeling?

Or because you weren't sure He loved you at all?

She squeezed Jeremy's hand. At least there was one thing she could say with absolute certainty. "Thank you, God, for Jeremy. Amen."

"Amen." Jeremy burrowed deeper underneath the covers.

"Now good night." Emma planted a kiss on his forehead and stood up. "We have to be at the library by eight tomorrow."

"Okay." He stifled a yawn. "'Night, Mom."

As soon as Emma closed the door, she sank against the wall and let the tears spill over.

"Well? How did it go?"

Jake sighed into the phone and heard Andy chuckle. "That bad, huh?"

"Define 'bad.'"

"But Emma didn't change her mind, right? She let you take Jeremy fishing."

"This time." Right up until the moment Jake put

the car into Drive, he hadn't been sure. He stepped out onto the deck and stared at the narrow strip of moonlight shimmering on the surface of the lake.

"Did the two of you get along?"

"Things were okay. Until I touched her—"

"Jake—"

"It wasn't inappropriate," Jake hastened to assure his younger brother. *The pastor.* "Her hair had come out of that little clip she wears and I just…"

Gave into the irresistible urge to see if it felt as soft and silky as it looked.

Jake gave himself another mental smack upside the head. If he wanted to earn Emma's trust, that hadn't exactly been the smartest way to go about it.

"Jake!"

"What?"

"I was asking if you and *Jeremy* got along," Andy said. "But if you want to talk about Emma, that's fine with me."

The undercurrent of laughter in his brother's voice warned Jake that he would never live this one down. "It's not what you think."

"What am I thinking?"

Jake's back teeth snapped together. "Can we *not* talk about Emma?"

"Sure," Andy said mildly. "But you're the one who brought her up. I was asking about Jeremy, remember?"

"Jeremy is a great kid." Jake grabbed at the opportunity to steer the conversation onto safer ground. "He didn't hold it against me that I promised to take him fishing and then, an hour later, I had to admit that I've never fished before in my life."

"That isn't entirely true, you know."

"I know you didn't believe this when I was *twelve,* and you probably aren't going to believe me now, but I wasn't trying to *catch* your goldfish," Jake grumbled.

"I found a string with a paper clip attached to it next to the aquarium. It doesn't take a background in law enforcement to figure out what was going on."

"Circumstantial evidence," Jake muttered. "And you accused *me* of holding on to the past."

"You do," Andy said without malice. "But I have things that God is working on, too. Which means we're both under divine construction."

That might be true, Jake thought, but he had a long way to go to catch up to his brother. The foundation of Andy's faith had been built long ago, before their parents had even met. Not for

Jake. God was starting from scratch with him. Most days Jake felt as if he were clinging to the cornerstone for strength, still surrounded by debris from the past.

"Jeremy would probably do better with someone who can answer his questions." And the boy had been full of them. In order to stop the flood, Jake had finally confessed that he was a new believer. But rather than being disappointed, Jeremy had seemed excited to discover they had something in common.

Go figure.

"If the Lord asks us to do something, He gives us the strength to accomplish it," Andy reminded him.

"See, that's what I'm talking about," Jake complained. "You always know what to say."

"Don't let the enemy convince you that you don't have anything to offer them," Andy had said right before he'd hung up.

At two-thirty in the morning, his brother's words cycled back through Jake's memory.

Offer *them?*

What had he meant by that?

He'd agreed to be a mentor because Jeremy needed someone willing to spend time with him.

But as Jake lay in bed, staring up at the ceiling, his thoughts drifted to Emma once again.

What did *she* need?

Emma didn't need this.

No matter how hard she tried to focus on her job, Jake kept invading her thoughts. And even when she wasn't thinking about *him,* the verse that Jeremy had read—*Jake's verse*—continued to play in her mind like the refrain of a familiar song.

Keeping her wayward thoughts in line proved difficult enough, but over the course of the day, Emma caught her gaze straying to the windows overlooking Main Street. In desperation, she began to contemplate rearranging the furniture in the library. Beginning with her desk.

By closing time, Emma couldn't wait to get home.

She locked the front door of the library and went to look for Jeremy. The last time she'd seen him, he had swiped a notebook and pen and disappeared into her office, a tiny cubbyhole located in the back of the building.

"Jeremy?"

"I'm over here, Mom," came the muffled reply.

She followed the sound of his voice to a corner

at the far end of the library and found him sitting on the floor with his back against the oversize book section. "It's almost time to close up. Are you ready to go?"

"Almost."

Emma hid a smile as Jeremy gave her a distracted smile. The notebook lay open on his lap and he continued to furiously sketch something on the page. She tilted her head but it was difficult to interpret the drawing upside down.

"What are you working on?"

"The design for our raft," Jeremy replied without looking up. "Jake said he would get the supplies if I drew up the plans."

Raft. Jake. Supplies.

Emma's knees suddenly felt a little weak. She anchored an arm against the K–O shelf for support.

"The two of you are building a...raft?"

"For the contest during Reflection Days next weekend. We're going to win, too, because I have a really good idea." Jeremy nibbled thoughtfully on the end of the pen. "The raft that makes it all the way to the flag and doesn't sink gets a trophy."

Be. Calm.

"And Jake thinks this is a good idea?" Emma's voice thinned out.

"Uh-huh." Jeremy blinked up at her. "I just need five more minutes to think, Mom. Is that okay?"

"Sure, sweetheart," Emma said between gritted teeth.

Five minutes would give her plenty of time to make a phone call!

Chapter Eleven

"Go away."

Jake froze in the doorway of the café, pinned in place by Kate's scowl.

"All I want is a cup of coffee." He tried to bluff his way past her suspicions, but someone must have gotten to Kate first. The Grapevine definitely lived up to its name.

"Sure." Kate snorted. "You don't want coffee, you want to upset the delicate balance of my life."

"Phil said you love animals."

"I do love animals," came the prompt response. "I'm what is commonly referred to as a 'cat' person. In fact, I have two of them. And they rule over a very small house. Did you ask Abby?"

"I called her first," Jake admitted. "She said she'd love to take him, but when she and Quinn get married, they'll have Mulligan and Lady out at the lodge." Jake didn't add that he blamed Quinn O'Halloran for giving Abby time to come up with an excuse. Quinn had seen the dog turning somersaults in the backseat of the squad car after Jake had picked it up.

A thoughtful look entered Kate's eyes. "A dog like that needs a home in the country. And kids. Having a pet teaches responsibility. But not someone too young," she added quickly. "Ten or eleven is a good age. You know what they say about the bond between a boy and his dog."

Was it his imagination, or had she put delicate emphasis on the word "boy"?

Jake's eyes narrowed. She couldn't be thinking what he *thought* she was thinking.

"You don't mean Jeremy Barlow."

"Jeremy Barlow." Kate clapped her hands together. "Wow, that's a great idea, Jake."

"Oh, no." Jake was already shaking his head. "I can't show up at Emma's with a dog."

Especially *this* dog.

The campaign Delia Peake had single-handedly launched to capture the animal that had been terrorizing her neighborhood had come to a successful, if not surprising, conclusion. In the interest of maintaining public relations—and because he knew the woman wanted to gloat—Jake had responded to the call.

Upon his arrival, Delia had risen to her full height of four feet eleven inches, which brought her nose even with his badge.

"Chief Sutton." The tip of her pink walking stick had struck the ground with each syllable. "I don't care what you do with that garden-destroying, Dumpster-diving creature as long as you remove it from my yard. Immediately."

If Jake had known what he was getting into, he would have sent Phil Koenigs instead. Standing guard over the garden-destroying Dumpster diver had become his assignment for the rest of the day. Along with finding it a temporary foster home until more permanent arrangements could be made.

"Jeremy is an only child," Kate said, building her case with the finesse of a seasoned attorney. "He would probably love to have a dog."

Jake knew she might be right, but at the moment, Jeremy wasn't the one he was thinking about!

"Do you know Emma at all?"

"No, and I feel bad about that." Kate's expression clouded. "I went to school with Brian. His death hit everyone pretty hard—nothing like that had ever happened around here before. No one had gotten to know Emma and because she was such a private person, we didn't want to intrude on her grief. Maybe that wasn't the best thing. For the town, or for her and Jeremy."

She poured a cup of coffee—in a travel cup, Jake noticed—and handed it to him. "None of us has been able to get close to her. You're the first person to get your foot in the door, so to speak."

"If I show up with that dog, Emma is going to slam the door in my face," Jake muttered.

"Maybe. Maybe not."

Jake was spared further comment when his radio crackled. "Excuse me."

"No problem." Kate flashed an impish smile before flouncing back to the kitchen.

"Chief?" Steve Patterson's voice came over the radio. "Emma Barlow called the department about twenty minutes ago. I told her that you'd checked out for the day, but Mayor Dodd noticed your car parked in front of the café."

"Emma called?" Out of the corner of his eye, he saw Kate smile.

"She asked to talk to you, but she didn't say why she was calling."

Jake ignored the blatant curiosity he heard in the officer's voice. "I appreciate you letting me know."

The only problem was, Jake thought as he slid the radio back into the leather holster on his belt, everyone else at the department would know, too. If they didn't already.

Kate's head popped up in the pass-through window between the kitchen and the old-fashioned soda fountain. "The library closed ten minutes ago. You could probably catch Emma at home. The home that happens to be located on a dead-end road."

"I know where Emma lives," Jake said drily. "But thanks."

"Helping local law enforcement is my civic duty," Kate intoned.

Jake waited until he was outside before he rolled his eyes at the sky.

Tag-teaming again, Lord?

He slid into the driver's seat and turned on the radio to drown out the ruckus in the backseat.

"Take it easy, back there." Jake tried to sound soothing in order to stop the howling but the only thing he managed to do was turn up the volume.

Who was he kidding? Emma would never agree to take the dog in.

But she *had* called the department and asked to talk to him. Had Emma changed her mind because he'd crossed a line? Upset the delicate balance of her life, as Kate would say.

At least that evened things out between them.

Emma Barlow upset the delicate balance of *his* life, too.

Call him a glutton for punishment, but Jake turned off on Stony Ridge Road anyway.

He parked the car in front of the house but instead of going up to the door, he followed the soft strains of jazz music to the stone silo near the barn, thinking that Jeremy might be playing inside.

"Jeremy?"

No answer.

Jake ducked his head and slipped through the narrow doorway. He was about to call out the boy's name again when he heard the sound of glass breaking.

All his instincts kicked into gear as he lunged through another doorway into a small room attached to the silo. Jake stopped short as a glass missile hurtled toward the wall and broke into a rainbow of colorful fragments.

It wasn't Jeremy that he'd found. It was Emma. Streaks of gray cement covered her bare arms and the faded denim overalls she wore. It looked as if she'd been playing in the mud. Sunlight streamed through the windows, sparking off the gold threads in her hair.

"In another situation, this could qualify as disorderly conduct, you know."

Emma whirled around at the sound of his voice.

"What are you doing here?" she gasped.

Jake sauntered over to the radio and stabbed the tip of his finger against the power button. "One of the officers said you called."

"Yes, but I didn't dial 911," Emma said tartly.

Jake laughed, not put off by her response. She looked too adorably rumpled to intimidate him. "I was on my way home and decided to swing by in person." He made a quick scan of the room as he spoke. An old wooden table, filled with baskets of broken glass and pottery, was centered along one wall. A pyramid of plastic buckets rose from a pallet in the corner. What the room lacked in space it made up for in natural light. A wall made up of tiny windows captured the sun like a prism.

"Is this your studio?"

"Nothing quite so lofty." Emma shook her head, the movement setting her ponytail into motion. "Like I keep telling Abby Porter, this is a hobby."

"Well, you're good at it." Jake studied the piece she had been working on. The top of a small, rather ordinary-looking table had been transformed with pieces of glass and colorful stone. At first glance, they seemed to be set into place with no particular thought or pattern. Jake looked more closely.

"It's the lake."

Emma stared at him in disbelief. "There's no blue in it."

"There doesn't have to be," Jake pointed out. "Water isn't always blue."

Without responding, Emma bent down and began to collect pieces of broken glass, the set of her shoulders an indication that Jake was once again guilty of trespassing. "You didn't have to drive over here," she finally said.

"I was on the way home. Your place isn't out of the way." Jake knelt down to help and the scent of strawberry shampoo teased his senses. "Did you need something?"

Yes, Emma thought. *I need you to leave me alone.*

Which didn't make sense, especially considering the fact that she was the one who'd contacted him. *By phone.* She hadn't expected Jake to stop by the house to talk to her in person. Or catch her in the middle of taking out her frustration on a box of innocent cups and saucers!

No one but Jeremy had ever seen her working on a mosaic. Not even Abby, who'd asked if some of her guests would be welcome to watch Emma work. Her response had been a polite but firm *no.*

Jake Sutton, as usual, hadn't waited for an

invitation. He didn't hesitate to intrude upon the private areas of her life—and her heart.

Emma tried to resurrect some of the anger she'd felt after her conversation with Jeremy. "It's about this...raft contest," she sputtered, rattled by his closeness.

"Jeremy is pretty excited about it." Jake shifted his weight, bringing them close enough for Emma to see delicate flecks of gold leaf embedded in the amber depths of his eyes.

Concentrate, Emma!

"I'm sorry." He blew out a sigh. "I did warn you that this is all new to me. If you don't mind me asking, why don't you want Jeremy to compete in the race? I asked around today and a lot of boys his age sign up."

But not *my* boy, Emma wanted to protest.

"He's never even watched the events, let alone asked to participate in one of them," she said instead. "I don't understand this sudden interest in something he never seemed to care about before."

A heartbeat of silence stretched between them. "He's been interested, Emma, but he never pushed the issue because he thought *you* wouldn't want to."

"How can you say that?" Emma surged to her feet, her tone accusing.

Jake raked a hand through his hair. "*I* didn't say it. Jeremy did."

Emma didn't know if she believed him. But maybe it was because she didn't *want* to believe him. "But I've never told Jeremy that I didn't want to go to Reflection Days. Why would he say that?"

"Maybe because Jeremy is as protective of you as you are of him."

The quiet response splintered what remained of Emma's composure.

Jake must have misunderstood. If Jeremy had wanted to go to the Reflection Days celebration, he would have said something to her. Besides that, she had never come out and said they couldn't go. She just hadn't…encouraged it. And Jeremy hadn't seemed interested.

She *knew* her son. She was sensitive to his personality. His interests. Jeremy was an introvert, similar in temperament to her, so when it came to extracurricular activities or social situations, Emma hadn't forced him out of his comfort zone.

Because it would have forced you out of yours, too?

Emma closed her eyes, blindsided by the realization that Jake's interpretation of the situation could be right.

All this time, she'd thought that she was being sensitive to what Jeremy wanted, but Jake claimed that her son had been doing the same thing.

Taking care of her, protecting her, was a burden that Emma had never wanted to put on Jeremy's shoulders.

But apparently, Emma thought with a stab of pain, Jeremy had placed it on himself.

"Excuse me." She walked past Jake and stumbled out of the building into the sunshine.

That went well.

Jake took a moment to mentally beat himself up for the clumsy way he'd handled things.

If only he'd had a clue that Emma's concern about the raft race had prompted her phone call. Jeremy had been so pumped up about the upcoming Reflection Days celebration, Jake should have known he would mention it to his mother.

It might have helped if you would have mentioned it, too, Jake silently berated himself.

The night before, while he and Jeremy had been fishing off Abby's dock, a boat had skimmed past. Mayor Dodd and two other members of the city council had been on it. The mayor had waved a bright yellow flag and jovially explained it was time to put it in the water and mark the halfway point for the raft race.

Noticing the way Jeremy's attention continued to stray from the bobber floating in the lily pads to the yellow flag flapping on a buoy offshore, Jake had asked if he participated in any of the events held during Reflection Days.

Making conversation, that's all he'd been guilty of. He hadn't expected Jeremy to say he'd never even *attended* the celebration that had become an annual tradition in Mirror Lake.

It hadn't taken Jake long to discover that Jeremy was in a tough spot, torn between not wanting to upset his mother and yet wanting to compete in some of the events.

He hadn't expected Jeremy to put him in a tough spot, too.

The boy had asked if Jake had ever been afraid to do something. When Jake admitted that he had, Jeremy asked if being afraid should stop a person from doing something.

Naturally, Jake had said no. More times than he could count, he'd faced dangerous situations in his line of work.

Jeremy's thoughtful nod had made Jake feel as if he were getting the hang of this mentoring thing. Until Jeremy's next question had blindsided him.

"Then can we enter the raft race together?"

Saying yes had brought an immediate smile to

Jeremy's face. Jake should have known that Emma would have a different reaction to the news.

Once again, he was going to have to convince her to trust him. If he could catch up to her. Emma was probably already in the house by now...

He strode outside and found her rooted in place, her gaze fixed on a point farther up the driveway.

She glanced at him, confusion replacing the pain he'd seen in her eyes a few moments ago.

"Is your car...moving?"

Chapter Twelve

Jake had forgotten about the dog.

How could he have forgotten about the dog?

At the moment, however, he was thankful for any distraction that had erased the stricken look from Emma's eyes.

"Yes, it is, but I'd keep my distance if I were you."

Emma ignored the warning and quickened her pace, forcing Jake to increase his stride to keep up with her.

"What is it?"

"Mrs. Peake's tomato-eating raccoon."

Now she stopped. "You put a raccoon in the *backseat?*"

"I couldn't exactly put it in the trunk. As tempting as that was," Jake added darkly. "Don't get too close—"

Emma reached the car and bent down to peer

inside the window. A furry body slammed against the glass.

She jumped backward, almost toppling Jake over. A pink tongue swiped the window in the exact spot her face had been.

"I know you're from the city," Emma said cautiously. "But that isn't a raccoon, Jake. It's a *dog*."

"Tell that to Mrs. Peake." Jake shook his head. "She ordered a live trap for 'troublesome wild animals' and she's convinced that's exactly what she caught."

The dog, in a blatant attempt to cultivate sympathy, began to whine. A thin, pitiful sound that had Emma stepping up to the window again. "It looks like a Lab mix."

"And sounds like it swallowed a siren." Jake winced. "I've been listening to that all day. I tried to bribe him with food, biscuits, a rawhide chew and a rubber ball but no deal."

"Do you know who he belongs to?"

"No idea or he'd be back home, safe and sound, by now. No one has reported a missing dog and this guy has been on the loose for over a week. He's either lost or abandoned." Jake had a hunch it was the second. He tapped on the glass but the mournful wail continued.

Emma pushed her fingers through the opening Jake had left in the window and fondled a silky ear.

The whining stopped. Just like that.

"What did you do?" Jake demanded.

"I think he wants some attention, that's all." She reached in farther to scratch the dog's other ear. "You can let him out while we wait for Jeremy to come out. He probably doesn't like being cooped up."

Jake hesitated, remembering the condition of his office after he'd had the same thought. "It's probably safer to leave him in the car. He's pretty wound up. I shut him in the storage room this afternoon and he tried to dig his way out."

"What are you going to do with him?" Emma wanted to know. "The closest animal shelter is almost an hour away."

Jake didn't want to be reminded. In spite of Kate's brilliant plan to pawn the animal off on Emma, he doubted that she would be willing to take him in.

"I'm going to bring him home with me for the night. Tomorrow I'll call around and see if there's an opening at a shelter."

"He's not going to like being in a kennel there, either."

Emma opened the door before Jake could stop

her. The dog shot out of the backseat as if someone had launched it from a cannon...and then dropped at her feet and rolled over.

Jake's mouth fell open.

"Definitely out of control." Emma's lips curved into a smile as she reached down to rub the dog's belly.

"He likes you."

"Don't be silly," Emma said briskly. "He likes attention."

"I gave him attention," Jake reminded her.

"You gave him toys."

Jake opened his mouth to argue...and then realized she was right.

"Hi, Jake!" The front door slammed and Jeremy bounded up, bypassing him and going straight for the animal lying prone at his mother's feet. "Cool! Is this your dog?"

"It's a stray I picked up today."

"A stray!" Excitement backlit the blue eyes. "Can't we keep him, Mom?"

Emma was already shaking her head. "He doesn't belong to us, sweetheart."

"But he doesn't belong to anyone else, either," Jeremy said reasonably. "So why can't we keep him?"

"I don't think that's a good idea."

"Why not?"

* * *

Why not?

Emma could come up with a dozen reasons. Well, at least two.

"You're starting school in a few weeks and I'm at work all day." Emma could tell she was weakening. Unfortunately, so could her son.

"How about a trial period?" Jeremy pushed. "To see if he likes us?"

Jake coughed but Emma knew he'd done it to hide a laugh. Emma's huff of exasperation covered one of her own. What was she getting into? She didn't even know if the dog was housebroken.

The dog licked her hand and whined, as if adding an appeal of its own.

"We're not really set up to take in a dog on such short notice." Emma scratched the furry muzzle and heard a contented sigh. "We don't have any dog food."

"I have a bag in the car." At her incredulous look, Jake lifted his hands. "Hey, it was either provide kibble or have holes eaten in the upholstery."

Emma raised an eyebrow. A comment like that was supposed to convince her to bring the dog into their home?

"It sure looks like he's settled down a lot, though," Jake said, immediately recognizing the error of his ways. "I don't think he's destructive. Like you said, he just needs some attention."

"I can give him lots of attention." Jeremy grinned up at her.

"We'll keep him for the weekend and see if we all get along. That's the only promise I'm willing to make." Emma only hoped she wouldn't regret the decision!

"I'll show him my room." Jeremy jumped to his feet. "Come on—" He looked at Jake. "What's his name?"

"You can do the honors." Jake lowered his voice. "I won't tell you what Mrs. Peake called him."

Emma hid a smile. Delia Peake served as the chairwoman of the library board. The woman had a backbone as strong as her pink walking stick.

"I'll think of one." Jeremy patted his leg. "Come on."

The dog looked at Emma, as if asking for permission. She wasn't fooled for a minute. This had to be some sort of conspiracy. She waved her hands. "Go on. You may as well let Jeremy take you on a tour of the place."

The dog rolled to its feet and grinned, the pink tongue unfurling like a ribbon.

"He knew what you said. He's smart, isn't he?" Jeremy said.

"He seems to be." Emma's eyes narrowed on

Jake. The smug expression on the man's face had her wondering if this hadn't been his plan all along!

"You might want to give him a dish of water," Jake suggested.

"You aren't leaving, are you, Jake?" Jeremy's worried gaze shifted from Jake to his mother.

"I'll stick around for a few minutes."

"Mom, can Jake stay for supper?"

"Jeremy!" Emma choked on the word.

Her son looked at her, wide-eyed. "What? I asked you first this time."

Out of the corner of her eye, Emma saw Jake smile. He would realize that she'd been backed into a corner and offer her a way out.

"I'm sure Jake already has dinner plans." *Please have other dinner plans.*

The glint in Jake's eyes told her that he'd read her mind.

"I'd love to stay."

"What are you two doing out there?"

Jake winked at Jeremy as he handed him another nail. "Tell her it's guy stuff."

"It's guy stuff, Mom."

"Guy stuff, hmm? That explains why it's so noisy." Emma's sigh was audible through the window screen. "Supper will be on the table in five minutes."

Jake had waited until Emma disappeared inside the house before asking Jeremy if he would like to assist him in a small project. Just as Jake had suspected, Jeremy was more than willing to help. He had led Jake to the barn, where a rusty box held the tools they needed.

He wasn't sure how Emma would react to him fixing the loose boards on the porch. Especially considering he'd already turned her day upside down by signing Jeremy up for the raft race without her permission. And dumping a stray dog into her lap.

"How does this look?" Jeremy sat back on his heels.

Jake surveyed his work. "One or two more whacks with the hammer should do it."

Twin lines of concentration plowed rows between Jeremy's eyebrows as he followed Jake's instructions. "Is this better?"

"It looks great."

Emma poked her head around the door. "Come in and wash up now."

"We're fixing some loose boards on the porch, Mom."

"I see that."

Something in her tone told Jake that his list of misdemeanors was growing by the minute.

They trooped inside and washed up at the kitchen sink. The house boasted no formal dining area but Emma had tucked a small oak table in the corner. The table had already been set for three, the floral china arranged just so. Not a paper plate or plastic fork in sight.

Jake sniffed the air appreciatively. A pan of lasagna served as the centerpiece, the cheese still bubbling around the edges. A basket heaped with garlic bread and a salad completed the meal.

The comfortable setting was so far removed from what he was used to, he wasn't sure what to do next. As an undercover drug officer, the places he'd called "home" over the past few years hadn't been the kind that encouraged people to linger. The furniture, what there was of it, reeked of cigarette smoke. Dishes would pile up for days, waiting until someone came down from their high long enough to do a cursory cleaning.

"You can sit here, Jake." Jeremy pointed to the chair next to his.

"As long as I don't have to share my garlic bread."

Jake had meant it as a joke, but when he glanced at Emma, the color had drained from her face, making her eyes appear even more blue.

"Is something wrong?"

"No. Please, sit down." Emma glanced at the chair that Jeremy had offered him. The one at the head of the table.

Brian's chair.

Chapter Thirteen

He should have known better.

If Andy called tonight, asking for details, his brother would probably contact Matt and have him removed from the team of mentors.

"I'll sit here instead." Jake pulled one of the other ladder-back chairs away from the table and sat down. "That way, I can fight you for the garlic bread *and* the salad." He winked at Jeremy.

"Okay." Jeremy grinned but didn't reach for either one. "Should we pray, Mom?"

Emma's head jerked up and her gaze collided with Jake's across the table. "You go ahead, sweetheart."

Jeremy closed his eyes. "Lord, thank You for this food and thank You that Jake could stay for supper. Thanks for Shadow and I pray that he likes it here. Amen."

Emma might have offered up a thank-you for the

food, but Jake wasn't sure she would have joined Jeremy in thanking God for the rest. Especially considering that he and the dog hadn't been on the guest list for the evening meal.

"You named him Shadow?" Emma looked up.

"He looks like one, don't you think?" Jeremy reached down and patted the dog on the head.

The dog's tail began to thump out a gentle beat against the floor, almost as if it approved of the name.

"He was as hard to catch as one," Jake said. "But he seems happy here."

If he didn't know better, Jake would have thought someone had switched dogs when his back was turned. The one who'd terrorized the police department all day now lay stretched out on the rug, the picture of contentment.

"I showed Mom the plans for our raft, Jake." Jeremy's smile glowed as bright as the candle burning in the center of the table. "We have to sign up for the race by Monday."

Emma's strong reaction to the raft race had left Jake hoping for another opportunity to discuss it with her. The last thing he wanted to do was undermine her authority as a parent.

"When we talked about the raft race last night, I assumed you had your mother's permission to enter," Jake said carefully.

Jeremy sank a little lower in the chair and peeked at his mother from beneath a thick fringe of sandy brown lashes. "Is it okay with you, Mom?"

Emma gave a short nod. "I suppose so. As long as Jake is willing to help you."

"He promised he would." Jeremy's expression shifted from relieved to anxious once again. "Didn't you, Jake?"

"Yes, I did." Jake was glad he could put the boy's mind at ease now that Emma had given her permission.

Jeremy passed the bowl of salad to him. "The first thing we have to do is build a model of my design to make sure it floats."

"Can't you just build the raft ahead of time?" Emma asked.

"Uh-uh." Jeremy shook his head. "That's one of the rules. You have to bring the stuff to make it and build it right there. And you only get ten minutes to do it. You can't use parts of a real boat, either. Or sails. You have to paddle them. Some of the rafts tip over right away because of the uneven weight distribution, but I know a way around that."

Jeremy paused to take a breath and Emma squeezed in another question. "How do you know so much about the race?"

"I've been thinking about it for a few years

now," Jeremy said matter-of-factly. "I just got tired of being afraid to *do* it. Jake said that being afraid shouldn't stop a person from doing the things they want to do."

Jake said.

The words hung in the air between them.

Great, Jake thought. Between the dog and the raft race, he'd probably worn out his welcome. The trouble was, he was in no hurry to leave.

He wanted to linger over the best meal he'd had in ages. And finish fixing the porch.

And spend more time with Jeremy and Emma.

While his head questioned whether he belonged there—with them—his heart seemed more than ready to make itself at home.

"You were afraid sometimes when you were undercover, weren't you, Jake?" Jeremy tucked into his lasagna, unaware of the growing tension at the table.

"That's right." Jake just hadn't expected it to come up again as dinner conversation!

Emma's eyes darkened in confusion. "But that was a long time ago, wasn't it? You must have had a desk job of some kind before you came to Mirror Lake. A patrol officer doesn't just skip to the rank of police chief."

She was right. But that "patrol officer" could

skip a few rungs on the department ladder when God had a hand in things.

"Technically, I held the rank of sergeant when I left my last job."

"But why did you move to Mirror Lake? Do you have family in the area?"

"No." The innocent question pinched a nerve. Jake had limited contact with his family when he'd agreed to go undercover, telling himself it was best for everyone that way. Andy had tried to set him straight at the time, but he hadn't listened. Rebuilding a relationship had come more slowly with his mom and stepdad than with his stepbrother. "Mirror Lake is the place I'm supposed to be. I believe that God brought me here for a reason."

And now that he'd met Jeremy and Emma, that reason was becoming a little more clear. From what he could see, Emma's grief had formed a protective wall around both of them for so long, it almost seemed as if they'd become trapped inside of it.

Emma's smooth brow furrowed. "You think that God cares about things like that?" she asked hesitantly.

Jake met her doubtful gaze head on. "I know He does."

"That's because God saved Jake when he got shot," Jeremy added helpfully.

Emma's fork clattered to the floor.

"You were…shot?"

Jake winced.

Yeah, come to think of it, he'd mentioned that to Jeremy, too.

Jake had been shot.

Shot.

Emma's gaze flickered to the crosshatch of scars on the underside of his jaw. Had a bullet grazed a path there?

The thought made her stomach pitch.

"No." Jake caught her staring. "I wish I could impress you with a heroic deed, but these particular scars were caused by stupidity." He scraped the back of his hand over the scars. "When I was eight years old, I decided to make a tree fort in the backyard."

"What happened?" Jeremy leaned forward, fascinated by the tale.

"It didn't work. I fell. But instead of landing in the sandbox, I bounced off the fence that separated our yard from the neighbor's. Mrs. Parker grew prizewinning roses." He winked at Jeremy. "But not that year. She also got the sympathy vote from my mother, which meant that I had to spend the entire summer weeding flower beds."

Jeremy laughed but Emma couldn't. She was still reeling from the knowledge that Jake had survived an injury much more serious than falling into a rosebush.

She excused herself from the table and went to get a clean fork. As it was, Jake saw too much—she certainly didn't want him to see the tears that had sprung to her eyes.

Tears that caused her doubts to surface once again. For the past six years, she had done her best to shelter Jeremy from the pain of losing his father at such a young age. Now, not only had she agreed to let Jake mentor her son, but she had just discovered that he was a living testimony of how dangerous his chosen profession could be.

Jeremy was already getting attached to Jake. Emma could see the hero worship in his eyes—hear it in his voice—whenever he talked about the man.

Jake had survived a gunshot wound once, but Emma knew from bitter experience that there were no guarantees he wouldn't be hurt again. Not even in a small town as idyllic as Mirror Lake.

How would Jeremy handle that?

How would you?

Emma pushed the unwelcome thought away.

This wasn't about her—this was about Jeremy and what was best for him. Wasn't it?

She walked back to the table, careful to avoid Jake's eyes.

"I think I'll take Shadow for a walk," Jeremy announced. "Who wants to come with us?"

"We should all go." Jake slanted a look at her. "After we help your mom clean up the kitchen."

Emma stiffened. She didn't *want* his help.

She didn't want to go for a walk, either. All she wanted was a few minutes alone to untangle the knot of emotions balled up inside of her.

"You two can go ahead without me. There isn't much to clean up." Emma sucked in a breath and held it, hoping Jake would take the hint.

"Jeremy, will you please take Shadow outside?" he asked. "I'll be there in a few minutes."

"Sure." Jeremy slapped his palm against his thigh. "Let's go, Shadow."

The dog launched to its feet and beat him to the door. Emma could hear Jeremy's laughter as it closed behind them. She should have gotten him a dog a long time ago, but she had always talked herself out of it.

"Supper was delicious, Emma."

"Thank you." She turned on the water and let the sink fill, acutely aware of Jake picking up the dishes and stacking them on the table behind her.

"No, thank you." His husky voice, and the fact they were alone, created a level of intimacy between them that should have made Emma uncomfortable. Especially after what she'd just learned.

It felt so strange to have him there, in her kitchen. Sitting at the table. Sharing a meal with them.

Emma had seen the understanding dawn in his eyes when Jeremy had offered him the chair at the head of the table. He must have assumed the look of shock on her face stemmed from the fact that she didn't want him to sit in Brian's chair. To take his place at the table.

But that hadn't been the reason. The truth was, Emma had suddenly realized that Jake's presence in her home, in spite of her misgivings, didn't feel wrong at all. In fact, somehow, it felt…right.

"No dishwasher?" Jake's voice rumbled close to her ear.

"No." A shiver danced its way down Emma's spine. "It isn't necessary for you to help me, you know."

Jake smiled. "I've already been in hot water a few times tonight… What's one more?"

In spite of the fact that she was struggling to find her next breath, Emma fought a sudden urge to smile. She covered it with a stern look as they switched places at the sink. "So you admit that it wasn't an accident, showing up with a stray dog?"

"I'll admit it was good timing." Jake rolled back the sleeves of his white dress shirt and began to wash the plates. "I had a dog and you had a ten-year-old boy who needed one."

Emma averted her gaze from the corded muscles of Jake's forearms. He'd locked his gun belt in the trunk of the car, but still wore his uniform shirt and badge. That—and the story about surviving a gunshot—provided vivid reminders of what he did for a living.

"You make it sound so simple."

Jake's shoulders lifted and fell. "Sometimes we complicate things."

And sometimes things got complicated without a person even trying, Emma thought. Like the feelings that Jake's presence in her home stirred up inside of her.

Feelings she didn't *want* to feel.

"Let me know the days you want to take Jeremy to work on the raft." She began to wipe down the countertop to put some distance between them.

"Like you said, Reflection Days starts next Friday, so you don't have a lot of time."

"I know." She felt the force of Jake's smile. "That's why I thought we'd build it here."

Chapter Fourteen

❧

"'Mornin, Jake. What got you out of bed so early on a Saturday morning?"

Jake, who'd been staring at a mind-boggling display of dog leashes and collars for the past ten minutes, turned at the sound of Phil Koenigs's voice.

A smile slid across the officer's weathered face when he noticed the yellow collar clutched in Jake's hand. "Don't tell me you ended up with that troublemaker? Aren't you supposed to delegate responsibility?"

Because it was Saturday, and they both happened to be off duty, Jake couldn't very well reprimand his second in command for insubordination. Although the grin on the officer's face definitely qualified.

"I did. And I found him a good home."

"No kidding." Phil glanced at the box of biscuits

and the Frisbee tucked under Jake's arm. "Then what's all this for?"

"A guilt offering." Or a bribe. Jake didn't care what it was called as long as it changed Shadow's status in the Barlow home from temporary to permanent.

"So where did you drop him off? The county shelter?"

"No, I gave him to Jeremy Barlow." Jake hooked the yellow collar back over the metal arm on the display and picked out a red one instead. "How big do you think he's going to get? Medium, large or supersize?"

"Emma took him?"

The strangled question pulled Jake's attention away from the collars.

"That's right." He glanced up in time to see a strange expression shift the broad planes of the officer's face. "What's the matter?"

"I'm just surprised, that's all," Phil muttered.

From Jake's standpoint, there was more to it than surprise. Aisle three in the local lumber store seemed as good a place as any to find out what it was. This wasn't the first time Phil had displayed obvious discomfort when Emma's name came up.

"I've been spending some time with Jeremy

through the mentoring program at Church of the Pines."

"Heard about that," Phil said shortly. "I just have a hard time believing that Emma agreed to it, is all."

He wasn't the only one, Jake thought. But that didn't explain why the senior officer couldn't seem to look him in the eye.

"Do you have a problem with Emma?"

Phil seemed troubled by the question. "Why do you ask?"

"Oh, I don't know," Jake drawled. "Maybe because you and the guys were drawing straws to decide who had to drop off a bouquet of flowers on the anniversary of her husband's death."

"It's more like Emma has a problem with us," Phil said. "I wish she would have moved away after...you know."

The admission stunned Jake. "Because it's difficult to see her still grieving?"

"Not only that." Phil shifted his weight as if adjusting the burden of guilt he bore. "We never did catch the person on the motorcycle that Brian was pursuing."

Jake let out a slow breath. "I'm sure Emma doesn't hold you or the other officers responsible for not making an arrest."

Phil didn't look convinced. "Brian and I worked

together on third shift at the time. He came over the radio and said he'd just clocked a motorcycle going ninety miles an hour. I told him to let it go. Department policy states that for safety reasons, we aren't supposed to pursue anyone at those speeds." A shadow passed through his eyes. "Brian always was a bit of a cowboy but I never thought he'd take off after the cycle anyway. When dispatch tried to call him a few minutes later, he didn't respond. The accident reconstruction team figured Brian lost control on a curve and rolled the squad car. He died on the way to the hospital. Maybe it would have given Emma some closure if we'd made an arrest. Maybe she thinks we should have tried harder. Or gotten help for Brian sooner."

The undercurrent of anguish in Phil's voice made Jake wonder if the officer was imagining that Emma blamed him—because he blamed himself.

"You did the best you could. In a situation like that, you can second-guess yourself until you go crazy." Jake spoke from experience, even though he wasn't always successful when it came to taking his own advice. No matter how many times Andy reminded him that he couldn't take responsibility for Sean's decisions, there were times Jake questioned whether the outcome would have been different if *he* had done something different.

"It happened six years ago and there are still nights I lose sleep thinking about it." Phil grimaced. "Even if Emma doesn't hold us responsible, I think it's hard for her to see the badge and not be reminded of everything she lost. She's very protective when it comes to her son. I guess that's why I was surprised she agreed to let Jeremy spend time with you."

Now that Jake knew more of the details surroundings Brian's death, he couldn't believe she had, either.

"There you are! I should have known you'd found someone to talk shop with." Phil's wife, Maureen, rounded the aisle, the warm look in her eyes belying her scolding tone. "Good morning, Chief. You're up bright and early on a Saturday."

"Hi, Maureen."

Phil looked relieved by the interruption. After a few minutes of small talk, he put his hand under his wife's elbow and guided her away.

As Jake drove to Emma's house, the conversation with Phil kept cycling through his mind.

The truth was becoming more and more difficult to deny. He didn't want Emma to see a badge when she looked at him.

He wanted her to see *him*.

"We need your help, Mom."

Jeremy dashed into the outbuilding, where

Emma was painting the legs on the mosaic table Abby had ordered.

When Jake had promised he would help with the raft, she hadn't expected him to show up at nine o'clock the next morning. At least he hadn't caught her sitting at the table in her pajamas, bleary-eyed while she waited for her first cup of coffee to take effect. She blamed the fact that she'd slept a little longer than usual on the amount of hours she had tossed and turned throughout the night.

No matter how hard she tried, she couldn't seem to dislodge Jake from her thoughts. And when he'd walked into the kitchen, looking way too attractive for her peace of mind in a pair of faded jeans and a butter-soft chambray shirt, Emma had bolted.

She'd been hiding ever since.

Fortunately, the table she was making for Abby provided a legitimate excuse to avoid the barn, the location Jeremy and Jake had claimed for their raft-building project. At least until now.

Emma rocked back on her heels. "What do you need me to do?"

"Time us," Jeremy said, holding up a stopwatch. "We're not sure how long it's going to take to put the frame together."

"I suppose I can do that," Emma murmured. "Let me wash up first and I'll meet you over there."

"Okay." Jeremy darted away, Shadow hot on his heels.

Apparently Jake had been right about that, too. A dog and a ten-year-old boy were made for each other.

Emma turned on the faucet and washed the paint off her hands. She was stalling, there was no point in denying it.

The fact that she wanted to see Jake made her *not* want to see him even more. And that kind of topsy-turvy thinking was proof of the effect the man had on her!

"Mom!" Jeremy's voice drifted through the open window. "Are you ready yet?"

"On my way." But only because she didn't have a choice in the matter.

Emma entered the barn and almost bumped into Jake, who was kneeling on the dirt floor. He rose to his feet and dusted his hands against his jeans.

"Sorry we had to interrupt you, but it's going to take both Jeremy and me to put this thing together and we needed a timekeeper. Shadow is very smart for a canine but I don't think he can help us out." Jake flashed that teasing smile, the one Emma had seen the day he'd slapped on the battered Stetson for story hour. The one that never failed to send her heart on a roller coaster ride to her toes.

Emma's fist closed around the stopwatch as she resisted the urge to reach out and brush a swatch of tousled dark hair off Jake's forehead. In plain-clothes, it was all too easy to forget what he did for a living.

Too easy to forget that, by his own admission, he'd been injured—no, not just injured, *shot*—while working undercover.

Jeremy hadn't seemed upset by the knowledge. Emma, on the other hand, hadn't been able to put it out of her mind.

Jake had talked about how God had led him to Mirror Lake at the same time and she wondered how he reconciled what had to be a horrific experience with his strong faith in a loving God.

In order to hide her troubled thoughts, Emma pretended to study the eclectic array of parts scattered on the floor at their feet. "Tell me when you're ready and I'll start the clock."

"We have ten minutes to assemble the raft," Jeremy told her. "But the longer it takes, the less time we have to paddle out to the flag. We need to figure out how to reduce the time."

"Jeremy thinks we can do it in six," Jake added. "I think he's right."

The grin on her son's face reflected a confidence Emma had never seen before—at least not until Jake Sutton had entered their lives.

* * *

"Do you think Mom will be surprised when she sees what we did?"

"No doubt."

No doubt whatsoever, Jake thought as he surveyed their work with a critical eye.

Once she had finished timing them, Emma had promptly retreated to her workroom again.

That had been two hours ago, and Jake hadn't seen her since.

He and Jeremy had spent the next hour working out some snags in the raft's original design before taking a short break. Taking Shadow for a walk around the house had given Jake an opportunity to take a silent inventory of a few of the more pressing repairs that needed to be finished before winter set in. He might not have much experience when it came to home handyman stuff, but he was willing to try.

If he could convince Emma to *let* him.

At the lumberyard that morning, Jake had picked up a few extra boards along with the supplies needed for the raft. Jeremy, eager to test out the brand-new junior tool set Jake had given him, didn't mind putting aside that particular project for a while.

"I'm finished with this one." Jeremy rubbed

his nose with the back of his hand. "Are you hungry?"

Jake could take a hint. "Are you ready for lunch?"

Jeremy leaped to his feet. "I'll get Mom."

"Your mom said something about finishing up a table for Miss Porter. How about we make lunch for her today?"

Jeremy considered the suggestion with the same thoughtful concentration he applied to other decisions. "I like hot dogs. Mom likes grilled cheese sandwiches and tomato soup."

"I think we can handle that."

"So do I." Jeremy grinned.

They straightened up the barn before walking back to the house. Shadow attached himself to Jeremy's side. Jake couldn't help but notice how quickly the pair had taken to each other.

The soft smile he had seen on Emma's face when she noticed the dog's brand-new collar had lingered at the edge of Jake's thoughts all morning.

Who was he kidding? Everything about Emma lingered in his thoughts, from the way her eyes darkened to an evening-sky blue when she was thinking hard about something to the gentle sway of her hips when she walked.

Grilled cheese sandwiches. Tomato soup.

Jake firmly rerouted his thoughts as they went inside.

"Mom usually does everything." Jeremy stood in the middle of the kitchen and looked at him for direction.

"Which is why we're going to give her a break today." Even as he spoke, Jake hoped Emma wouldn't show up until lunch was ready.

But she did.

She ventured into the kitchen less than ten minutes later. Jeremy was standing at the counter, buttering slices of bread, while Jake kept a watchful eye on the tomato soup.

Her cheeks flushed a delicate shade of pink. "Why didn't you come and get me?" she scolded them. "I would have made lunch."

"We wanted to surprise you." Jeremy inserted a piece of cheese between two slices of bread before carefully transferring it to the skillet.

"You did." Emma sidled into the kitchen. "I'll set the table."

"Already done," Jake said.

Emma glanced at the table and the uncertain expression tugged at his heart.

She took care of Jeremy, but when was the last time someone had taken care of her?

"There must be something I can do," she persisted.

"There is." Jake pointed to the table. "You can sit down. You've been working hard all morning."

Emma didn't listen. She wedged her way in between them and her gaze flickered to the wooden spoon in Jake's hand.

He lifted it above his head. "Don't even think about trying to disarm a police officer."

Jeremy giggled.

"I wasn't." Her blush deepened.

"Uh-huh." Jake let his skepticism show.

"I can't see the pan, Mom, 'cause you're in the way." Jeremy heaved a sigh.

"Sorry." Emma stepped back. "I guess I'll just…"

"Sit down." Jake and Jeremy said the words at the same time.

Emma laughed. "All right, all right. I'll sit down."

The unexpected sound rippled through the kitchen—and snatched the air from Jake's lungs.

Breathe.

"The sandwiches are smoking." Jeremy's announcement jump-started Jake's heart again. "Does that mean they're done, Jake?"

"Affirmative. And they look great." Jake ignored the crispy dark brown edges—*his fault*—as he flipped the sandwiches onto a plate. "I told you we could pull this off."

"Jake made tomato soup for you, Mom." Jeremy took the carton of milk out of the refrigerator and poured three glasses. "I told him you liked it."

"Hot fudge sundaes and tomato soup." Jake set a bowl down on the colorful woven place mat in front of Emma. "If you aren't careful, pretty soon I'll know all your secrets."

"That means I'll have to be careful then, won't I?"

Jake had been teasing. One look at Emma's guarded expression told him that she hadn't.

"I'll say the prayer today." Jeremy slid into his chair at the table and bowed his head.

Jake listened as the boy thanked God for the soup and grilled cheese sandwiches. And Shadow. And that they had put the raft together in a record-breaking seven minutes and thirty-four seconds.

After Jeremy's "amen," Jake tacked on a silent prayer of his own.

Thank You for showing me there is still laughter inside of Emma. Keep working in her heart. Show her that You haven't forgotten about her. That You love her.

Jake opened his eyes and found Emma staring at him. For a split second, all her defenses were down. He saw bewilderment and confusion—and a longing that both terrified him and gave him hope, all at the same time.

Or was what he was seeing in Emma's eyes simply a reflection of his own emotions?

Chapter Fifteen

Over the swish of the washing machine, Emma heard the muffled but steady tap of a hammer. Only this time, the noise wasn't coming from the barn. It wasn't coming from the porch, either, where Jake and Jeremy had fixed several loose boards the day before.

She would have thought Jake had projects of his own to attend to on a beautiful Saturday afternoon, but he seemed to be in no hurry to leave.

An image of him standing next to Jeremy in the kitchen, patiently supervising his efforts, surfaced in her memory again. Jake claimed to have no experience with children and yet he instinctively seemed to know exactly what would appeal to a boy like Jeremy, who wanted to learn new things.

Emma had shooed them out of the kitchen after lunch, assuming that Jake would take the hint. He and Jeremy had taken Shadow for a walk instead.

She stepped outside and followed the tapping to the back of the house.

Emma wasn't sure what she'd expected to find, but the sight that greeted her momentarily stopped her in her tracks.

Jeremy sat cross-legged in the grass next to the back door, paintbrush in hand. The screen door had been removed. So had the screen, which someone had wadded up and stuffed into a garbage can.

Her gaze flew to Jake. He stood several feet away from Jeremy, hands propped on his lean hips as he stared up at the misshapen metal gutter that followed the roofline.

"I thought you two would be back in the barn, trying to shave a few more minutes off your time." Emma couldn't help the fact that her statement sounded like an accusation.

Both heads turned in her direction.

"We're taking a break," Jeremy explained.

"You're taking a break to *work*." Emma planted her hands on her hips. "I don't think I've ever heard of that."

He waved the brush at her, inadvertently spattering the grass with droplets of white paint. "Jake bought a new screen for the door."

"Did he?" Emma pinned a look on Jake that should have drawn another response other than the smile he flashed in return.

"I noticed the old one had a few holes in it," he said.

Fixing the back door had slowly been working its way up the project list, but Emma wasn't sure if she should be grateful or embarrassed that Jake had noticed its pitiful condition.

"He bought me my own set of tools, too." Jeremy pointed to a toolbox gleaming in the afternoon sunlight, as shiny and red as a McIntosh apple.

"That was nice of him." Too nice. Except that Emma didn't want Jake to feel obligated to buy Jeremy gifts. Or give up an entire Saturday to work on projects that weren't his responsibility.

They weren't his responsibility.

"I made some lemonade." Emma manufactured a smile for Jeremy's sake. "Jeremy, why don't you bring the pitcher and some glasses out to the picnic table and take a *real* break?"

"Okay." Jeremy jumped to his feet and transferred the paintbrush into her hand before disappearing into the house.

Emma quickly maneuvered the dripping brush over the can.

"It's primer." Jake sauntered over, not looking the least bit guilty at having been caught in the act of another home-repair project. "I wasn't sure if you wanted to repaint the frame the same color, so I didn't pick up the paint for that yet."

Yet.

"You're Jeremy's mentor, not my carpenter."

Jake stuffed a rag in the back pocket of his jeans and shrugged. "A boy should know his way around a toolbox."

So that's what this was about. Another "teachable moment."

The things she had sheltered Jeremy from, like hot skillets and hammers and raft-building contests, Jake considered learning opportunities. Emma couldn't deny that she had liked it better when Jeremy had learned things from a book, but she couldn't deny that her son's confidence had been steadily growing.

"How much do I owe you for everything?"

"Nothing." Jake's jaw tightened.

"I can't let you pay for the supplies." Emma folded her arms across her chest and raised her chin. Jake would discover she could be just as stubborn as he was. It was bad enough he had taken it upon himself to make repairs, she couldn't let him absorb the cost.

"All right." He gave in. "If you insist."

"I do."

"The cost of the supplies is dinner."

"D-dinner?" Emma stammered.

"Jeremy mentioned that you make great home-made pizza. And since I don't specialize in home-made anything, that would be reimbursement enough."

"Pizza? That doesn't seem like a fair trade." And opening her purse would be easier on Emma's peace of mind than opening her home to Jake again.

"It's more than fair. Jeremy wants to help you. It gives him a sense of pride," Jake said.

Pride? What about her pride?

Emma was embarrassed by her inability to keep up with simple outside home repairs—and morti-fied that Jake had noticed.

Her gaze strayed from Jake to the siding that was practically begging for a fresh coat of paint.

"I've thought about selling the house." Emma couldn't believe she had said the words out loud.

Jake was silent for a moment, as if he'd been sur-prised by the admission, too. And then, "Did you and Brian live here while you were married?"

Emma nodded, surprised that the mention of Brian's name didn't flood her with painful mem-ories. "It belonged to his grandparents. After Grandma Barlow died, Brian's grandfather closed up the house and moved to Arizona to live with Brian's parents. When Brian took the job with the Mirror Lake police department, his grandfather was thrilled. He called the house a wedding gift."

"A difficult one to return," Jake commented.

Emma couldn't argue with that.

"It was supposed to be temporary." Regret stirred the ashes of Emma's grief. "We planned to build a place on the lake eventually, but Jeremy was born premature and couldn't leave the hospital for two weeks. The bills piled up and it seemed wiser to stay put until we got back on our feet."

Their five-year plan.

She and Brian had had such a short amount of time together, Emma sometimes felt as if she had never really gotten to know her husband at all.

"Brian didn't have any other family close by?"

"An older sister, Melissa, but she had already graduated from college and moved to the east coast by the time we got married." Emma, who had always dreamed of having a sister, had been disappointed that Brian's only sibling had moved so far away. "She writes at Christmas and sends Jeremy a birthday card every year, though."

The shadow in Emma's eyes ignited a slow burn that worked its way through Jake as the truth became clear.

The very people who should have been there to lift her up had, in fact, let her down.

"Don't Brian's parents, or his sister, ever come back to visit?" he asked carefully.

Emma shook her head. "There isn't anything here for them anymore."

There's you, Jake wanted to say. *And Jeremy.*

From the way Emma described her situation, it sounded as if she and Jeremy had been… abandoned.

"I don't blame them," Emma said quickly, as if she'd read his mind. "The memories… It would be hard for them to come back here."

"You stayed."

"I didn't have much of a choice." Emma shrugged. "The house might have come with some flaws but at least it didn't have a mortgage. When Jeremy turned two, I started working a few hours a week at the library, just to supplement Brian's income a little, but after…" Some of the strength in Emma's voice ebbed away. "When Mrs. Morrison retired, she suggested that the library board offer me the full-time position because I had experience, even though I hadn't finished my degree."

"What about your family?" Jake felt compelled to ask.

The silence that fell between them lasted so long

that Jake didn't think Emma was going to answer the question at all.

"My mom died in a car accident when I was six years old," she finally said. "Dad was in the military, so we never stayed in one place very long. After I graduated from high school, I decided to take some classes at a local technical college. The next time Dad moved, I was an adult, so he moved without me."

"Where is your father now?"

"He retired a few years ago but accepted a part-time job as a consultant with a civilian company overseas. He only makes one trip back to the States a year."

Which answered the next question that had begun to form in Jake's mind.

Something in his expression must have shown, because Emma stepped back. The guarded look returned.

"I'm sorry. I didn't mean to go on and on."

And she didn't want him to feel sorry for her, either. But Jake didn't. He felt sorry for all the people in Emma's life who had never taken the time to get to know her.

"Don't be sorry. It will help me get to know Jeremy better if I know some of his background." Jake spoke the truth but the brief glimpse into Emma's past had told him a lot about her, too.

But it was clear she was already regretting it.

"I read the guidelines for the mentor program that Pastor Wilde sent to me," Emma said slowly. "They state that mentors agree to spend four hours a week with the boy they've been assigned to. *Four hours.* You've put in your time and then some. I know you're busy. Please don't let Jeremy pressure you into spending more time with him than necessary."

"In the first place, I don't think of Jeremy as someone I've been *assigned* to," he said. "And I don't spend time with him because I feel pressured. I enjoy spending time with him."

And with you.

"It's nice of you to say that."

For some reason, the polite words rankled.

"Nice?" Jake repeated the word with a bite that caused her to flinch. "I'm not just saying it, Emma, I mean it."

He could tell by the expression on her face that she didn't believe him. "You said that you worked undercover," she said stiffly. "I realize that making grilled cheese sandwiches and fixing screen doors don't exactly provide the adrenaline rush that you must be used to."

"You're right about that," he agreed. "I slept on a lot of couches in houses that weren't exactly the picket-fence type. Saw things that I wish

I could forget." *Had done things he wished he could forget.* "I volunteered to work undercover because I wanted to change things, but I got in so deep. I didn't realize that I was the one who was changing, until I…until God got hold of me.

"Fishing with Jeremy. Listening to him laugh. Making grilled cheese sandwiches. Fixing the loose boards on your porch. Those aren't ordinary things to me, Emma. They feel more like a…a gift."

Chapter Sixteen

"Come on, Mom! It's almost time for church to start!"

"I'll be down in a minute." Emma felt a stab of guilt, knowing she wouldn't mind walking into the service a few minutes late. Then she and Jeremy could sit in the back row and avoid the fellowship time that took place in the foyer before the service began.

And Jake.

The conversation they'd had the day before came rushing back. Somehow, in the space of a few minutes, he had managed to coax her into revealing details about her life that she had never told anyone else.

Emma flushed at the memory. Jake Sutton hadn't charmed or forced his way through her defenses, either. Oh, no. One look into those mesmerizing amber eyes and she had practically invited him in!

Emma had reminded Jake about the mentoring guidelines in an effort to put some distance between them, but he had turned the tables on her.

"Those aren't ordinary things to me, Emma. They feel more like a gift."

She had been stunned by the sincerity in his voice. And the tiny current of awareness that had sparked the air between them. One that should have made Emma retreat rather than coax her to move closer.

Fortunately, the connection was broken when Jeremy, needing help carrying the pitcher of lemonade, called for help. Jake had opened the door for him—and provided Emma with an escape hatch.

He hadn't followed her that time. An hour later, from the safety of her workroom, she heard his car drive away. Emma had been able to breathe again.

At least for a little while.

The Sunday worship service would make another encounter with Jake inevitable, but a little distance, Emma reasoned, would give her a chance to put their relationship back into perspective.

Not *their* relationship.

Emma caught herself. She and Jake didn't have a relationship. They had an...an *agreement*. An agreement born from their commitment to Jeremy. He was the connecting point between them.

That's all it was.

"And it's enough."

If she said the words out loud, Emma thought, maybe she could convince her heart to believe them.

She drove into the church parking lot and Jeremy stuck his head out the window, his gaze scanning the rows of vehicles.

"I see Jake's car!" His entire body rose off the seat in his excitement. "Maybe he's waiting for us."

Emma hoped not. She could already feel a blush heating her cheeks at the *thought* of seeing him again.

As it turned out, they were a few minutes late. The worship team had taken their place at the front of the sanctuary and the young woman at the keyboard had started to play the opening notes of a popular praise song.

Emma released the breath she'd been holding. They could find a seat in the back...

"I see a spot!"

Before she could blink, Jeremy was hiking down the center aisle, his destination the second pew from the front.

The pew where Jake was sitting.

The trouble was, unless Emma wanted to draw even more attention than they already were, she had no choice but to follow.

Jake had already risen to his feet by the time Jeremy reached his side. He must have heard Jeremy's voice—Emma had no doubt *everyone* in the sanctuary had heard Jeremy's voice—because everyone in the row was shifting to make room for them.

Emma kept her eyes focused straight ahead as she took her place next to her son. It was clear that she was going to have to have a talk with him—and apologize to Jake. He may have agreed to be her son's mentor, but it didn't mean he was obligated to give Jeremy all of his attention.

Pastor Wilde stepped behind the podium to open the service with a word of prayer, saving her from further embarrassment.

During previous services, Emma had been able to retreat into herself—planning the next week's menu or silently sifting through the books in the research section of the library. But she hadn't had Kate offering to share her hymnal. And the words of the songs about God's love hadn't touched a bittersweet chord inside of her before, filling the empty spaces that had been there as long as Emma could remember. Even before Brian's death.

By the time Pastor Wilde finished his sermon and the congregation rose to their feet for the closing song, it was all Emma could do not to bolt from the sanctuary.

She did manage to sidestep Kate in her haste to get to the door, but found her path blocked by Esther Redstone. The elderly woman belonged to a knitting group that held their monthly meetings in the conference room at the library. Whenever they burst through the door, toting bags of yarn and enough food to feed a small army, Emma thought they looked more like a troop of Girl Scouts on a camping trip rather than a knitting group.

"There you are, Emma!" The woman's friendly smile made her a tiny but formidable obstacle. "Do you have a minute to chat?"

Over the woman's chic little straw hat, Emma saw Jeremy trudging toward the car.

"Of course." Emma couldn't say no. Esther exuded a warmth and beauty that rivaled the blankets she and the Knit-Our-Hearts-Together ministry created.

"Would you be interested in donating several of your mosaic garden stones for our booth at the craft show during Reflection Days next weekend? The proceeds go into a special Christmas fund for the missionaries the church supports."

Emma hesitated a moment before telling the truth. "I don't usually sell my work."

Esther wasn't deterred. "I know that, dear, but when the committee met last night, Abby thought you might make an exception this time."

Abby. Emma should have known.

"When is the craft show?"

Esther's eyes began to sparkle like sapphires. "Reflection Days starts on Friday afternoon and the craft show is one of the highlights of the kickoff. We set up tents near the pavilion at the park."

"How many do you need?" Emma asked, even as she silently calculated how much free time she would have that week and how long it would take to design and create an order of stepping stones.

"I don't know. One, two, three…" Esther peeked at her under the brim of her hat, sudden mischief dancing in her eyes. "A hundred."

In spite of her initial hesitation, Emma couldn't help but chuckle. "I don't think I could make a hundred in less than a week."

"Then we'll take as many as you are willing to donate," Esther said promptly. "I'm glad Abby thought of you. Thank you so much."

"You're welcome," Emma said automatically, even as she wondered at what point she had actually agreed to make the donation!

Esther patted her hand. "We could really use your help setting up that day, too. Kate mentioned that the library closes early on Friday afternoons."

So Kate was part of the conspiracy, too.

"Mrs. Redstone—" Emma gasped, the argument she was about to make cut off by the older woman's brief but exuberant hug.

"Wonderful! And please call me Esther, dear. No need to stand on ceremony when we'll be working together, is there? I'll see you at the pavilion at one o'clock on Friday afternoon." Esther released her and sailed down the hall.

Emma gave up. If necessary, she could let Kate or Abby know that she wouldn't be available to help. Since they'd been the ones who'd drafted her, they could find a replacement for her!

Making her way across the parking lot, Emma braced herself to face Jake again. They hadn't spoken after the service. Pastor Wilde had motioned to him after the closing prayer and Emma had immediately been caught up in the wave of people moving up the aisle.

But when she saw Jeremy, he was alone.

Emma resisted the urge to look around. "Are you ready to go home?"

"Uh-huh." Jeremy slid into the passenger seat.

On the drive back home, Emma could no longer resist asking, "Did you talk to Jake?"

"A little bit." Jeremy was staring out the window, so Emma couldn't tell if the conversation had been a disappointment.

"He has plans for this afternoon?"

"Uh-huh." Now Jeremy turned to look at her, eyes shining. "He's coming over for pizza."

Maybe, Jake thought, he shouldn't have accepted Jeremy's invitation to join him and Emma for lunch.

But then again, he *had* made a deal with Emma. Home-repair supplies for homemade pizza. And the truth was, even if Jeremy hadn't approached him after the service, asking when they were going to work on the raft again, Jake would have been hard-pressed to stay away and give Emma the space she wanted. Especially now that he was beginning to question whether "space" was what she *needed*.

The brief glimpse into Emma's past had left him shaken.

No wonder it was difficult for her to reach out to people and ask for help. Her family had never reached out to her. No wonder she was so protective of Jeremy. No one had protected her.

Her husband's family, locked in the grip of their own grief, hadn't been there for Emma after Brian's death. And from what Jake had learned about her father, his obvious indifference to her when she was a child had continued after she was an adult.

But it wasn't just the fact that no one had walked beside Emma through the pain of her loss, but the matter-of-fact tone in which she'd talked about it that stirred up Jake's anger. As if she hadn't expected it to be any other way...

"Jake?"

He felt a tug on his arm and found himself looking into a pair of wide, gray-blue eyes.

"Sorry, bud." Jake mentally shook himself. "What did you say?"

"I think I should ask Mom to time us again."

"You know what I think?" Jake looked down at the raft. "I think it's time we put this thing in the lake and take it for a test run."

Jeremy's eyes widened. "Really?"

"We have to make sure it floats, don't we?" Jake winked at the boy.

"Yes!" Jeremy pumped the air with his fist.

Jake smiled at his enthusiasm. "I'll check it out with your Mom first, before we start loading up the car." He had learned that particular lesson the hard way.

Jeremy had already dropped to his knees and began to dismantle the raft again, not concerned that they might not be granted permission to carry out the mission.

Jake, however, had his doubts.

Emma hadn't said much when he had shown up for lunch after church, but she had mentioned Esther's request that she donate some of her garden stones to the craft show.

He sensed a conspiracy. And if his suspicions were on target, Jake could have hugged Esther. The women were finding ways to gently coax Emma out of her shell.

Jazz music drifted through the open window of the outbuilding as Jake approached.

"Emma?" He called out a warning before entering her work zone this time. He'd learned that lesson, too.

"Come in."

"Are you sure it's safe?" Jake paused in the doorway and looked around for flying dishes.

"I'll tell you when to duck. Maybe."

Jake felt the air empty from his lungs.

Emma was teasing him? Because Jake could have sworn he saw a smile lift the corners of her lips before she looked down at the mosaic she was working on.

His gaze skimmed over her slender frame. Jake had thought Emma stunning in the dainty little sundress she'd worn to church that morning—he had barely been able to take his eyes off her. But she looked equally as fetching in tennis shoes, baggy overalls and a faded gray T-shirt.

Focus, Sutton. You interrupted her for a reason, remember?

"Do you mind if I take Jeremy down to the boat landing for an hour or so? We're satisfied that we've got a good time making the raft, now we need to make sure it's going to hold us."

"All right."

"All right?" he blurted, a little shocked that she'd agreed so quickly. After all, he was asking her to trust him. Again.

"I realize you have to make sure it's…sea-worthy." Emma pushed a piece of glass into the wet cement, adding to the row she had been working on.

But Jake didn't miss the little frown that settled between her brows.

It occurred to him that Emma was used to

spending her free time with Jeremy. Jake didn't want to be the guy who took her son away from her.

"We could use a spotter," he said casually. "It's a beautiful afternoon. Hot and sunny. I've heard a nasty rumor there might not be many of those left."

The frown deepened. "I have to finish this before the cement dries."

"We can wait."

Emma looked out the window at the cloudless sky. "I'll meet you by the car in fifteen minutes."

"I knew it." Jake flashed an approving smile. "The woman is beautiful *and* sensible."

Emma stared at Jake's retreating back as he sauntered out the door. It closed quietly behind him and she sagged against the table.

Beautiful.

In stained bib overalls and battered tennis shoes? Her ponytail trailing between her shoulder blades like a damp rope?

And sensible.

Emma turned the words over in her mind.

She caught a glimpse of her reflection in the antique mirror over the sink. The woman looking back at her was smiling.

Oh. No.

That morning, she had been trying to come up with ways to avoid Jake. Now, when she would have had the perfect opportunity, she had agreed to accompany him to the lake.

What was wrong with her?

She had been afraid that Jeremy was getting too attached to Jake. Now she had to wonder if she was guilty of the same thing.

Chapter Seventeen

"Stopwatch?" Jeremy looked over at her and Emma held it up for his inspection.

"Check."

"Camera?"

"Check." She dug around in her beach bag and produced that, too.

"Oatmeal cookies?" Jake took up the questioning, his teasing smile playing havoc with her pulse.

Emma made a face at him, knowing that he was remembering the picnic basket she had sent along on their first fishing trip.

"Chocolate chip," she whispered. "And they're for later."

"I think we're ready, Mom. Count to three and then say go," Jeremy instructed.

Emma took a deep breath, heart still suffering the aftershock from Jake's smile. "One, two, three...go."

She watched in fascination as the two of them set to work with an efficiency that made every movement look as if it had been choreographed. In a little over six minutes they were transporting the raft down to the shoreline, ready to launch.

Emma followed, keeping an eye on the stopwatch. According to Jeremy, the winner of last year's competition had completed the entire race— from start to finish—in five minutes and eleven seconds.

Jeremy clambered aboard but when Jake jumped on, the raft tipped to the side, threatening to capsize them.

"What's the matter?" Emma stopped at the edge of the water where the waves licked at the tips of her bare toes.

"Too much weight," Jeremy called over his shoulder.

"Hey!" Jake pretended to look affronted at the suggestion. "Keep paddling. She'll stay afloat."

But "she" didn't.

One of the barrels came loose and started to drift away, upsetting the balance even more. By the time they admitted defeat, both were soaking wet. They slogged back to shore where Emma was waiting with dry towels.

And the camera.

When the flash went off, Jake and Jeremy swung accusing looks in her direction.

"That wasn't supposed to happen." Jake reached for the towel.

"Really? The raft wasn't supposed to sink?" Emma saw their disgruntled looks. And giggled.

"Mom, you aren't supposed to laugh at us," Jeremy grumbled.

"I'm not laughing." Emma clapped a hand over her mouth to muffle the sound.

Jake arched a brow at Jeremy. "Sounds like she's laughing to me."

"Me, too." Jeremy began to dry his hair but they heard a low but unmistakable chuckle from beneath the towel.

"Oh, well. Back to the drawing board." Jake peeled off his shirt and Emma's breath hitched in her throat as she stared at his bare chest. Not at the ridged torso, as smooth and golden-brown as teakwood, but at the crisscross of raised, angry-looking scars just below his rib cage.

Jake realized what he'd done when he heard Emma stifle a gasp.

Now that the pain of his injury had, for the most part, subsided, he no longer thought about the scarring.

Until now.

He grabbed the extra shirt he'd brought along and shrugged it on, fumbling with the buttons in his haste to cover up the wound again before Jeremy noticed it.

Unfortunately, it was too late for Emma.

She stepped between him and Jeremy, using her body to shield his injury from curious eyes, but not fast enough for Jake to miss the mixture of shock and disbelief in her own.

Emma knew he had been shot, but Jake supposed there was a difference between knowing it had happened and witnessing the results.

Would she let him explain?

Jake blew out a sigh as he acknowledged there was a bigger question.

Could he explain?

Other than Andy and Pastor Matt, not many people outside Jake's former precinct knew the details surrounding his injury. That was the way he preferred it.

In silence, they loaded the pieces of the raft into the trunk of the car.

"What's up?" Jake caught a glimpse of Jeremy's pensive face in the rearview mirror.

"I thought for sure it would float," he said. "My calculations should have been right."

"Well, I happen to know one thing you didn't

calculate." Jake decided to take a page from Emma's book and try to help Jeremy see the humor in the situation.

"What?"

"You didn't add in the calories from the four slices of pizza I ate for lunch." Jake patted his flat stomach. "I'm sure that I weigh five pounds more than I did this morning."

That drew a smile.

"I ate that many, too," Jeremy confessed.

"So now we know. None of your mom's homemade pizza before the race."

Jeremy smiled, his earlier cheerfulness restored. Emma, on the other hand, didn't. Not only that, she had barely spoken a word since they'd left the park.

Jake had a hunch he knew the reason why.

By the time they arrived back at the house, the sun had started to set, outlining the trees in liquid gold. Shadow was waiting for them, wet nose pressed against the window and looking unhappy at having been left behind.

"Should I take Shadow for a walk?" Jeremy asked.

Emma shook her head. "It's getting dark. I can do it. You should take off those wet clothes and jump into the shower."

Jeremy obeyed but paused halfway up the steps.

"Are you coming over tomorrow after you get off work, Jake?"

Jake opened his mouth to answer but Emma beat him to it.

"Jeremy." Her voice was firm. "I'm sure Chief Sutton has other things that need his attention."

Jake winced inwardly. So they were back to his title again.

The boy's expression fell. "I guess so."

"Good night." Jake reached out and gave Jeremy's shoulder a comforting squeeze. "You do what your mom says and I'll put the raft back in the barn."

He was stunned when Jeremy's arms circled his waist and he hugged him before disappearing into the house. "G'night, Jake."

Emma appeared more troubled than surprised by the boy's unexpected display of affection.

"I'll unload the car," Jake said. "Shadow isn't going to let you forget that you promised him a walk."

She gave a brief nod and struck out across the yard, the dog streaking ahead of her.

Jake couldn't prevent a sigh from escaping. When it came to getting to know Emma, he felt as if he were on a treasure hunt.

The journey wouldn't always be easy, but he had

no doubt it would be worth the effort if he didn't give up.

He wanted to hear her laughter. He wanted to see hope dispel the grief in her eyes. There were times he caught a glimpse of those things and knew God was at work in Emma's life.

If he—and his career—stopped getting in the way.

If only the scars on his chest could be explained away with a lighthearted story about a tumble into the neighbor's rosebush.

By the time Jake unloaded the last pieces of the raft from the trunk of the car, it was dark enough that he was forced to turn the lights on in the barn. He started to straighten things up and then chided himself for lingering, knowing that Emma wouldn't seek out his company.

He turned to leave and that's when he saw her. Perched on an old wooden chest just inside the door, knees drawn up against her chest. Jake hadn't even heard her come in.

He closed the distance between them and dropped down beside her on the bench. Emma continued to stare straight ahead, the flickering overhead light illuminating the delicate lines of her profile.

Silence stretched between them.

Jake didn't know what to say. Wasn't sure what Emma wanted to hear.

"Who did that to you?"

The soft question broadsided him. If Emma had asked *how* it happened, he would have given her an abbreviated version of the events that unfolded the night of the drug bust.

But she hadn't asked "how." She had asked "who." And that complicated the situation.

"I don't like to talk about it." An answer that wasn't an answer.

"Then tell me about your family."

"I don't—" Talk about them either, Jake started to say. Until he remembered that he had asked Emma the same question the day before.

Let her get to know you, Andy had said.

Jake decided to take his younger brother's advice, especially if it meant that he could avoid talking about his injury.

"I have a mother and a stepfather. A younger stepbrother."

"Andy," Emma murmured.

Jake couldn't hide his surprise that she knew his brother's name. "That's right. But up until six months ago, I could count on one hand the number of times I visited them over the past five years. And I lived in the same city." Jake paused, waiting for the stab of regret to subside. "I didn't see them on holidays. I didn't stop by for coffee on the weekends."

"I don't understand."

Neither had they, Jake thought.

"Usually when an officer is undercover, he does some surveillance, makes a few buys until an arrest is made. My assignment lasted almost five years. In order to prove that I was one of them, I had to fit in. Had to earn their trust. It wasn't easy but it was…necessary…to do my job."

"So you had to sever ties with your family?"

"I thought it was in their best interest," Jake explained. "We weren't just trying to shut down a few neighborhood drug dealers. This was bigger. It went all the way to the top of the food chain."

All the way to police department.

All the way to Sean.

Emma felt, rather than saw, a sudden memory that ripped through Jake. Made him shudder. Did he even realize that one of his hands had moved to his chest, covering the scars she had seen that afternoon?

"Is that how you got hurt?"

"Yes."

When it didn't appear that Jake was going to offer any more information, Emma was forced to ask another question.

"They figured out you were a police officer?"

"Only after someone told them that I was." Jake closed his eyes briefly. "The night of the bust, two people died. I was supposed to be one of them. I was viewed as a threat—the other guy, Manny, he was...dispensable. A nineteen-year-old addict who'd been on the streets since he was twelve. He liked to brag that he only looked out for himself. He refused a direct order to shoot me."

"What happened? After...Manny?" Emma had to know. Not for her sake, but for Jake. Something in his eyes told her that this wasn't a memory easily shared.

She understood. She had a few of her own.

"Something that I can't explain other than to say that God intervened."

"Intervened?"

"I got hit and went down. That was the first bullet. The second one jammed in the chamber." Jake stared ahead with unseeing eyes, as if caught up in the memory again. "When I was at the end of my strength, I called out to God. He reached out His hand and He hasn't let go of me since."

Bile rose in the back of Emma's throat. Not only because a young man had lost his life, but because Jake had come so close to dying.

"The person who shot you?" she whispered. "Did they arrest him?"

"The SWAT team heard the first shot and they took the second one."

"And the person who set you up? Did you find out who it was?"

"Sean O'Keefe." Jake's eyes darkened with fresh pain. Pain that Emma sensed didn't have anything to do with his injury.

"You knew him?"

A heartbeat of silence followed.

"He was my best friend."

His best friend.

Emma swallowed hard. Without thinking, she reached out and covered the hand that rested on his knee. Jake's fingers curled around hers.

"Sean used our friendship to keep tabs on me and he knew that I suspected some of the officers were taking bribes to look the other way. I never expected he was one of them, though." Jake drew in a ragged breath. "The dealer didn't think I'd live to see morning, so he decided to make me suffer a little before he killed me. He told me everything. How Sean betrayed me. And why."

Their eyes met and Jake must have seen the question in hers. "It wasn't just for the money. I think he got tired. Disillusioned. The things a cop sees can wear him down. Tempt him to give in rather than fight. I wonder sometimes…" His voice trailed off but Emma knew what he'd been about to say.

"You wouldn't have." She could say the words with absolute certainty.

Jake's hand tightened around hers. "There were days when things got...blurry. When I was undercover, I walked a fine line between right and wrong in order to earn people's trust. There were times I stepped over it. It wasn't as hard to forgive Sean as it was to forgive myself for not realizing what was happening to him."

"But you did."

A smile lifted the corner of Jake's lips. "With God's help. I'd surrendered my life to Him, but when I was in the hospital Andy warned me that anger and bitterness could keep me stuck. Prevent me from moving forward. He was right. The weeks after Sean was arrested were a struggle, but I had made a promise to God the night I was shot."

"A promise?"

"To do things His way. To follow where He leads."

"To Mirror Lake." Emma remembered what Jake had said the night that Jeremy had invited him over for dinner.

"Andy agreed that it would be a good place to heal."

"Have you?" she asked without thinking. "Started to…heal?"

Jake rose to his feet with an enigmatic smile. "A little more every day."

Chapter Eighteen

"The garden stones are beautiful, Emma!"

"What did I tell you, Esther?" Abby breezed into the booth with an armload of afghans. "She has a gift."

"Abby." Emma knelt down to adjust a canvas flap—and to hide her embarrassment.

"She's right." Esther smiled. "Some of the people who wandered through earlier this morning asked me if you took orders."

"Mmm." Abby tossed Emma a "so there" look over her shoulder. "I brought some flowerpots from the inn so we can display the stepping stones as if they're in a garden. We can even have them leading up to the booth."

"That's a great idea." Esther nodded approvingly. "Emma? What do you think?"

Emma glanced at Abby and any reservations

she may have had were overcome by the infectious sparkle in the other woman's eyes.

"It *is* a great idea," she agreed.

"I'll be right back. The flowers are in the back of my car."

Abby dashed off and a white paper stick topped with a gigantic puff of spun sugar was thrust under Emma's nose.

"Cotton candy?"

Kate had returned.

"I can't. Just looking at that makes my teeth hurt," Emma confessed.

"But it will make your taste buds sing." Kate grinned. "Where did Abby run off to so fast?"

"She went to get the flowers." Esther poked her head out from behind the curtain of the booth.

"What can I do?"

"Someone made a last-minute donation," Esther said. "The church van is filled with crocheted pot holders that we need to find a place for."

"I'm on it." Kate saluted her with the cotton candy before handing it to Emma.

"I wish I had half that girl's energy," Esther said as Kate bounded toward the parking lot.

Emma raised an eyebrow. "You do."

"There are days these old bones wouldn't agree with you." Esther began to drape the afghans over the rungs of the antique wooden ladder Abby had set up in a corner of the booth.

Emma opened one of the boxes on the grass and pulled a brightly colored knitted blanket out. "Who made this one? I love the pattern."

"I did," Esther said. "And between you and me, I had more trouble with it. I must have started over a dozen times. Almost gave up that many, too. The only reason I stuck it out was because my grandmother designed the pattern. She's the one who taught me how to knit."

"I would like to buy this one," Emma said impulsively. "If you don't mind selling it to me, of course."

"Sorry." Esther was already shaking her head. "I can't sell it to you."

"Oh—"

"But I will give it to you. As a gift."

"Esther, no. I would rather pay for it."

Esther considered her for a moment. "I suppose you would," she said at length. "But I don't sell my afghans to friends, I give them away. That's another thing my grandmother taught me."

Friends.

Emma offered a tentative smile as she hugged the blanket against her chest. "Thank you."

"You're welcome." Esther looked pleased as she finished arranging the display of afghans. She turned her attention to the garden stones Emma had brought over to the park after work. "You do beautiful work, too. Did your mother teach you how to do this? Or did you take a class?"

"I taught myself. It's just a hobby," Emma said. "Something to fill the hours after Jeremy goes to bed."

Esther acted as if she hadn't heard her. One gnarled finger traced the uneven fragments of glass in the design. "Broken pieces of pottery— something that most people wouldn't see any value in—is used to create something new and beautiful. I look at these and I'm reminded that God does the same thing in our lives when we trust Him."

The words, soft as they were, cut Emma to the core. Maybe that was why she couldn't prevent the words that spilled out.

"I'm afraid to trust Him."

Emma couldn't believe she had said the words out loud. She glanced at Esther, knowing she would see disapproval. Or disgust. What kind of terrible person admitted that they were afraid to trust God? The creator of the entire universe?

But there was neither disapproval nor disgust on Esther's face. All Emma saw was understanding. And maybe a glimmer of humor. "Then I suggest you tell Him that."

Emma choked. "I can't!"

"You think it would surprise Him? When we tell God how we feel, we aren't telling Him anything that He doesn't already know." Esther smiled. "I love the story of the father who came to Jesus and asked Him to heal his son. The man tells Him that he believes—and in the very next breath, he asks Jesus to help him overcome his unbelief. He realized he didn't have a lot of faith but he knew who to turn to for help. That prayer was heartfelt. Honest.

"You want Jeremy to be honest with you, don't you? Not only do you want to laugh with him, you want him to come to you when he's hurting or upset. To share his heart with you. That's the kind of relationship God wants to have with *His* children."

Emma's throat swelled.

Her ten-year-old son had said the same thing the night they had prayed together. If only she could have that kind of faith. Simple. Uncomplicated.

Not at all like life.

She had always felt so…alone. Her father had treated her as if she were excess baggage he was obligated to haul from place to place. Other than those brief years with Brian, as long as she could remember, she had been alone.

"I just don't understand *why,*" she whispered.

Esther's eyes filled with tears. "You can tell Him that, too."

Jake spotted Emma talking with Esther Redstone in one of the craft booths set up near the pavilion.

Caught up in the whirlwind of pre–Reflection Days preparations, he hadn't seen much of Emma over the course of the week. The few times he had stopped by the house to spend time with Jeremy, Emma had been in her workroom, making stepping stones for the craft show.

Or had she been avoiding him?

Jake hadn't meant to share so many details about his past. If his goal was to get Emma to see beyond his badge, he'd made a mess of it. All he had done was give her more reasons to keep him at arm's length.

Keep working in Emma's heart, Lord. I'll try to stay out of the way.

"Are you avoiding her?" Kate had managed to sneak up on him.

Jake didn't bother to feign ignorance. Not with Kate. "No."

"Is that the whole truth and nothing but the truth?" Abby appeared beside her friend.

He'd been ambushed.

"I can arrest you both for disturbing the peace." Jake scowled. "My peace."

Abby's smile remained serene. "You are welcome to bring Emma and Jeremy over to the lodge tonight to watch the water parade. We've got the best view from the beach."

"Did I say I was going to the water parade?"

"Everyone goes to the water parade," Kate informed him.

"Everyone but Emma," Jake pointed out.

"Maybe no one's ever asked her."

Jake's eyes narrowed. "Emma doesn't like social events. I doubt I could convince her."

Especially now.

Kate grinned. "Mmm. If I remember correctly, that's what you said about the dog."

"Jake invited us to go to the water parade with him tonight. It's going to be awesome, Mom." Jeremy flopped down on the grass beside Emma. "Miss Porter is going to let us watch it from her dock and she's going to make s'mores and everything."

"Is she?" Emma shot "Miss Porter" a look.

"That's because Miss Porter's bed-and-breakfast happens to have the best view of the parade." Abby, busy arranging pots of autumn mums in front of the booth, didn't appear the least repentant.

"Can we go?"

"I don't know," Emma hedged. "I'll have to think about it. The parade doesn't start until ten. That's a late night."

"Think of it as a last hurrah before school starts," Kate interjected. "There's a bonfire at the park before the parade. A lot of people pack a picnic supper and make an entire evening of it."

"The water parade is beautiful." Esther joined the chorus. "Some of the business owners get quite creative."

"Thank you." Kate dropped a curtsy and grinned. "The Grapevine did win first place in the most original category last year. The girls from my book club have been helping me decorate the float this year. And I need all my friends to cheer us on."

"See, Mom?" Jeremy's expression became earnest. "Kate needs us."

"That's right. Kate needs you." The café owner aimed a saucy wink at Emma.

"Jake's never seen the parade before, either," Jeremy added for good measure.

Everyone waited expectantly for her decision.

"It looks like I'm outnumbered." Emma sighed. "You can go."

Jeremy's smile dimmed. "But he wants both of us to watch the parade with him. He said so."

Emma wasn't so sure about that.

Several times during the week Jake had stopped over after work to help Jeremy with the raft, but he hadn't exchanged more than a few polite words with her.

Not for the first time, Emma wondered if Jake regretted telling her about his friend, Sean.

After he had left that night, Emma had stayed in the barn for another hour, thinking about what he had said. He had a reason to be angry. Bitter. Instead, he had turned to God. Gave Him credit for being able to release those feelings and move forward.

Emma moved over to one of the tables, her hands unsteady as she began to rearrange a display of stained-glass suncatchers.

If she were honest with herself, she knew that she had been holding on to those same kind of feelings. Six years had gone by since Brian's death but she was afraid to look ahead. Afraid that if she did, she would forget him. Afraid that if she let go of her grief, she wouldn't have anything else to hold on to.

He reached out His hand and He hasn't let go...

Jake's faith stirred up that familiar longing again. Was it that simple? Reaching out to God and trusting that He would be there?

"Mom?" Emma felt a tug on her arm and realized that Jeremy was still waiting for an answer. "I don't want to go to the parade without you."

"I'll go along. If you're sure that Jake invited both of us."

"He said he'd find the perfect spot for the three of us to watch the parade. And you're one of the three of us," Jeremy said.

"You can't argue that logic," Kate murmured.

Abby clapped her hands together. "And I can help you find that perfect spot to watch the parade!"

Chapter Nineteen

"Jake's here!"

After two weeks, Emma should have been getting used to hearing the familiar refrain but her heart reacted the same way every time.

"Don't forget your sweatshirt," she called as her son streaked past.

"I won't."

Emma forced herself to take a deep breath. It was silly to become rattled over the thought of spending the evening with Jake.

"Look what Jake got for us!" Jeremy had returned, only this time he was waving a T-shirt over his head. He thrust it into her hands. "Isn't it cool?"

Emma examined the garment. It boasted wide red, white and blue stripes. But mostly red. Emblazoned on the front in bold block letters were the words TEAM VICTORY. "Wow."

"I know. It's for the race tomorrow." Jeremy could barely contain his excitement.

"It looks a little big," Emma murmured.

"That one is yours." Jake sauntered into the kitchen.

"Mine?" The word came out in a squeak.

"I had one made for each of us."

"Wow." Emma said it again.

"I'll bet none of the other teams are going to have shirts like this," Jeremy said.

"Probably not," Emma agreed.

Jake winked at her. "You can thank me later."

"I..." Emma forgot what she'd been about to say, her thoughts dissolving in the warmth of his smile.

"What's the matter, Mom?"

"Nothing." Nothing that she could explain, anyway. Emma grabbed her purse. "We better get going."

Jake took one look at the line of cars lining the driveway at the lodge and figured Abby had invited the entire town, not just a few friends, to watch the parade from her property!

"Abby is amazing," Emma said, her gaze sweeping the landscaped grounds in disbelief. "She should have entered a float in the parade."

"She didn't have to," Jake said as he followed

Emma across the yard. "Look at how many lights she used."

Luminaries hung from the branches of the trees around the lodge and white lights had been strung on the boathouse. The smell of a campfire permeated the air, dispersed by the warm breeze blowing across the lake.

As if on cue, their hostess breezed up to them.

"There's lemonade and cookies on the picnic tables," Abby said. "You can sit anywhere you want to but I promised that I would share an inside tip. The best view of the parade is from that little rise over by the cabins."

"Really?" Emma flicked a glance in that direction. "I don't see anyone else over there."

"That's strange," Abby said, the picture of innocence. "I guess you'll be the first ones."

Why did Jake have the feeling they would be the *only* ones?

"Thanks," he said drily.

She flashed a sunny smile. "Anytime, Jake. Now, I have to help Quinn make the s'mores. If you need anything, let me know."

Abby disappeared in the direction of the campfire, leaving the three of them alone again.

"There's Cody." Jeremy pointed to a shadowy figure waving to them from the end of the dock. "Can I go and talk to him for a few minutes?"

Emma didn't hesitate. "All right."

Jake wanted to hug her. He had noticed a tentative friendship spring up between Jeremy and Cody Lang and he wanted to encourage it. It looked as though Emma did, too, and was willing to put aside some of her reservations to let the boys get to know each other better.

"I'll be over there," she added, pointing to the spot Abby had suggested.

"Okay." Jeremy headed down to the lake and Jake fell in step with Emma as she moved toward the secluded spot under a circle of towering white pine.

He hadn't expected her to accept his invitation to the parade, but suspected Jeremy had had something to do with her decision.

Which was why Jake had asked him first.

There was a burst of applause as the first float in the parade chugged around the curve of the shoreline. Strings of multicolored lights fastened to a frame transformed the ordinary fishing boat into a coffee cup, complete with a curl of "smoke" fashioned from strips of filmy white cloth that fluttered gently in the breeze.

"Look! That one must be Kate's."

Jake smiled at the note of excitement in Emma's voice. He spread the blanket out under the tree. "Here you go."

"Thank you." Emma sat down on the edge of the blanket, her gaze riveted on the line of boats as they came into view. "I had no idea so much work went into this."

"Neither did I." Jake stretched out beside her. "Mayor Dodd stopped by the department so many times this week, checking on this and that, I considered deputizing him."

"He came into the library a few times, too. I think he wanted to make sure I hadn't taken down any of the posters."

Two more floats brought a loud chorus of oohs and aahs from the spectators on the beach.

"Sounds like they're having fun," Jake commented.

"You don't have to keep me company, you know," Emma said quietly. "I'd understand if you'd rather join the party."

"I am right where I want to be." It was the truth but Jake wondered if he'd said too much.

There had been a few times when they were together that he imagined feeling a spark of attraction between them, but Jake had convinced himself that's all it was. His imagination.

He reached for the thermos of coffee and his arm brushed against Emma's. She shivered.

"Are you cold?"

"N-no."

That didn't sound very convincing. Jake stripped off his denim jacket and draped it over her shoulders.

The coat almost swallowed her whole.

"Well, at the moment you look more like Sheriff Ben than Chef Charlotte." Laughing, Jake slid one hand underneath the frayed collar to free her hair. She had worn it loose today and it slid like satin between his fingers.

His laughter faded away. Without thinking, Jake cupped the back of her head in his hand and pulled her closer. Their lips met in a fleeting but gentle kiss that turned Jake's heart inside out.

A split-second after he let her go, he saw the shocked look on Emma's face.

"I'm sorry." Jake released her. "I don't know why..." *Yes, you do.* "Excuse me a minute. I think I'll check on Jeremy."

He surged to his feet.

There'd been times he'd had to face a difficult situation and calmly stand his ground.

This wasn't one of them.

"What time is it?"

"Twelve-thirty." Jake padded to the sliding glass door and stared outside. "Were you sleeping?"

"Yes. Now my question is, why aren't you?" Andy yawned.

"I just got back from the water parade a little while ago."

"Ah." His brother sounded more awake now.

"What does that mean? *Ah?*"

"It means you were with Jeremy and Emma Barlow."

"They'd never seen it before." And he had sure made it a night to remember, Jake thought wryly.

"You're spending a lot of time with them."

"I'm Jeremy's mentor. That's kind of the point."

"So where does Emma fit?"

Jake had a mental image of wrapping Emma in his jacket. Pulling her into his arms. And the look of shock on her face...

He groaned.

"Uh-oh." Andy's voice was laced with amusement. "What did you do this time?"

"Nothing. I'd rather not talk about it."

"No talking about nothing. Got it." Another yawn. "You have feelings for Emma, don't you?"

"Andy." Jake gave a warning growl.

"Oh, that's the nothing you don't want to talk about. Sorry. I'm a little slow at...twelve fifty-three in the morning."

Jake rolled his eyes even as a smile worked at the corners of his lips. "Why did I call you?"

"Because you miss me," Andy said promptly.

Jake shook his head. "I'll let you go back to sleep."

"Jake?" Andy's voice became somber. "God is in control, and I don't say that because it's written in a pastor's handbook somewhere. He brought you to Mirror Lake for a reason and it wasn't an accident that you met Jeremy and Emma. Trust Him. And get some sleep. Isn't that big raft race you've been telling me about tomorrow morning?"

"Eleven o'clock."

"Let me know how it goes."

"Thanks, Andy."

"Anytime, Bro."

Jake hung up the phone and got ready for bed. He lay down, linking his hands behind his head as he stared up at the ceiling. As usual, his kid brother was right. He did need to trust that God was in control.

And he did have feelings for Emma.

Lord, I know You're at work in my life and in Emma's. I don't know what's going to happen, but I do trust You.

The next time Jake woke up, it was because his pager was going off.

* * *

Emma woke up and found two pairs of eyes staring at her.

One blue, one chocolate brown.

"Are you awake, Mom?" Jeremy whispered.

She smiled, reminded of the Christmas mornings when Jeremy would sneak into her bedroom before dawn and ask the same question. "I am now." Emma covered a yawn. "What time is it?"

"Six."

"Six?" She sat up and Shadow took that as an invitation to launch himself onto the bed. He turned a circle and flopped down, propping his chin on her feet.

"The pancake breakfast starts at seven, remember?" Jeremy plopped down next to the dog.

Emma groaned. She couldn't believe a town the size of Mirror Lake could pack so many activities into one three-day weekend. "I remember. But we don't have to be the first ones in line, do we?"

"How about the second?" Jeremy summoned the heart-melting smile that she had never been able to refuse. "Do you think Jake will be there?"

Emma's heart flipped over. "I'm not sure, but he'll be at the park in time for the raft race. Why don't you take Shadow for a walk while I get dressed and have a cup of coffee?"

At the word walk, Shadow's ears lifted.

"Go on, now." Under the blankets, Emma nudged the dog with her toe. Shadow jumped down and followed Jeremy out of the room.

She collapsed back against the pillow and closed her eyes.

Jake had kissed her.

And she'd *wanted* him to.

That was what had taken her by surprise when Jake had drawn her into his arms.

There was no denying the truth any longer.

She had reluctantly let Jake into her life…and over the past few weeks he had somehow worked his way into her heart.

The day promised to be a warm one, so Emma dressed in denim capris and a lightweight floral shirt. There was no sign of Jeremy and Shadow when she came downstairs but a cup of coffee sat on the counter, cooling.

Ordinarily, the thought of attending any kind of social event, being surrounded by people, would have put Emma on edge. Filled her with dread. But this felt different. She was looking forward to seeing Esther Redstone. Listening in on Kate and Abby's lively banter. Watching Jeremy interact with some of the boys he'd met at church.

And seeing Jake again.

"Are you ready, Mom?" The screen door banged

behind Jeremy and Shadow as they skidded into the kitchen.

"Ready to eat cold pancakes and sausage at a picnic table outside?" Emma grinned. "Can't wait."

Jeremy responded to her teasing with a grin of his own. "Don't forget the camera so you can take pictures of me and Jake at the race."

"I won't." Emma had already stashed it in her purse the night before. "If Shadow has food and water, I guess we're ready to go."

Shadow walked over to his dog bed in the corner and collapsed with a sigh, as if he knew he wasn't invited along on this particular trip into town.

"Do you have your T-shirt, Mom?"

Her T-shirt.

Emma gulped. "I'm not sure where I put it."

"I think it's in the laundry room on top of the dryer," Jeremy said helpfully.

So it was. Bravely, Emma pulled the shirt over her head and avoided the mirror in the front hall as she walked out the door.

The short drive to Mirror Lake seemed to take a lot longer than usual.

"I can't believe people get up this early on a Saturday morning," Emma muttered as she drove around the parking lot for the second time, trying to find an empty space.

"It's the pancakes, Mom. And people want to be here early and get a good spot to watch the race."

Emma finally found a narrow space between two pickup trucks and eased her car between the painted lines. Jeremy would have bailed out immediately, but she put her hand on his arm.

"Wait a second, Jeremy. I want to talk to you about something."

In spite of his eagerness to be the first one in the breakfast line, Jeremy settled back against the seat. "What is it, Mom?"

"The race." Emma wasn't quite sure how to proceed. "I don't want to discourage you, but you are competing against teams who do this every year. I just don't want you to be too disappointed if you don't win."

"I know. Jake told me the same thing."

Emma blinked. "He did?"

"Yup. Jake said it doesn't matter if we win or lose, that we had a lot of fun building the raft and that's the most important thing."

Jake said.

The very words that Emma had once thought of as a threat now made her smile. "I guess that's covered, then."

"*Now* can we eat pancakes?"

"Now we can eat pancakes."

They made their way over to the line of portable buffet tables, where Kate was doling out plates.

"You two are up bright and early this morning." She smiled as Jeremy almost danced through the line.

"*Jeremy* was up bright and early this morning," Emma corrected. "He's excited about the race but I'm surprised he didn't sleep longer, considering how late he was up last night."

"Last night," Kate mused. "The water parade was beautiful. Did you see it?"

"Of course I did. You were there…" Emma's voice trailed off when she caught Kate's not-so-subtle meaning.

"All I'm saying is that from my vantage point, it looked to me like you were watching someone—I mean *something*—else."

Emma almost smiled. "I'm leaving now."

"You can run, but you can't hide." Kate's lilting voice followed Emma's retreat. "Nice shirt, by the way!"

As Emma searched for a place to sit, she spotted Esther Redstone and Abby sitting together under the pavilion. Abby immediately waved and patted an empty spot on the bench beside her.

"Over here, Emma! We saved a spot for you and Jeremy."

The sweetness of the gesture stripped away any

apprehension that Emma had been feeling. They lingered over breakfast and cups of hot coffee. More people began to arrive and Emma glanced at her watch, surprised to see that over an hour had passed.

There was still no sign of Jake, but she wasn't worried. A few of the teams had begun to assemble down by the lake, but he and Jeremy would have plenty of time to set up before the start of the race.

After they finished eating, Abby left to track down Quinn, who'd volunteered to help with security. Emma decided to check on Jeremy, who had gone to the playground with Cody Lang.

Jeremy broke away from the group. "Is Jake here yet?"

Emma scanned the people setting up lawn chairs along the beach. A flutter of uneasiness skated down her spine.

"Not yet."

Chapter Twenty

"He'll be here." Jeremy didn't look the least bit concerned that the start of the race was drawing closer.

"Let me check my cell phone. Maybe he tried to call." Emma opened up her purse and fished around inside but all that turned up was her checkbook, sunglasses and a tube of lip gloss.

In her haste to leave, Emma realized she must have left her phone on the nightstand.

"Is there anything I can help you with?"

"We can unload the trunk now, I guess." Jeremy looked around. "The other teams are starting to get ready."

Daniel joined up with them on the second trip to the car and helped them carry the rest of the supplies down to the beach.

"Well, folks, the annual raft race will be starting shortly." Mayor Dodd, armed with a microphone on the makeshift stage, boomed out the announcement. "You may want to grab a lawn chair and make your way down to the lake. This event is a Reflection Days tradition and we've got two more teams signed up this year…"

Abby drew Emma to the side. "What's the matter?" she whispered.

For Jeremy's sake, Emma had tried to hide her concern over Jake's continuing absence. But the race would be starting in less than half an hour and it was getting more difficult not to panic. If Jake didn't show up, Jeremy would have to forfeit.

"Jake should be here by now." Emma kept her voice low so Jeremy wouldn't overhear. "I left my phone at home, so I don't know if he tried to call."

"Here. You can borrow mine." Abby retrieved her cell phone from the tapestry bag looped over her shoulder.

"Thank you." Emma took a few steps away and dialed the number. Out of the corner of her eye, she saw Abby whispering something to Quinn. Her fiancé glanced at Emma and nodded before he strode away.

Emma closed the phone and handed it back to her. The question in Abby's eyes had Emma shaking her head. "There's no answer."

By quarter to eleven, the mayor bellowed a first call to the teams signed up for the race.

Jeremy wilted against her side, eyes bright with unshed tears even as he struggled to keep a brave face. "I don't think Jake is coming, Mom."

Emma tamped down her rising panic. "Don't worry, sweetheart. We have a few minutes yet. He'll show up."

He *had* to show up.

Five minutes later, however, she was beginning to doubt her own words.

"All teams should begin to line up behind the yellow tape." The announcer's cheerful voice came over the loudspeaker.

"I'm sorry, Emma." Abby's soft voice barely cut through her panic.

Anger rose up inside of Emma, weaving through the anxiety that had already tied her stomach into knots. Jeremy had been counting on Jake. So had she. What was she supposed to tell her son? That all the time and effort he had put into planning for the race had been for nothing?

Abby squeezed her arm. "What should we do?" Her expression mirrored the helplessness that Emma was feeling.

"I think we can make room on our raft." Quinn stepped forward. "Jeremy can race with me and Cody."

Emma felt a tug on her arm and looked down at her son's face. The tears were still there...but so was a look of determination.

"Did you hear Mr. O'Halloran?" Emma tried to keep her tone upbeat. She couldn't let Jeremy see how upset she was by Jake's absence. "He offered to let you race with them."

"Thanks, but that's okay." Jeremy flashed a shy smile at Quinn even as he turned down the invitation.

"Two minutes!" the mayor bellowed.

The onlookers moved closer together on the beach, the noise subsiding into a hushed anticipation.

"Jeremy, you're under thirteen. The rules state you have to have an adult with you," Emma reminded him.

"I know. You can go with me."

Emma's knees buckled. "Me?"

"We can do it, Mom." Jeremy sounded so confident that Emma almost believed him. "You watched me and Jake put the raft together a million times."

Not even close, Emma thought wildly. It had been three or four at the most, every time they'd asked her to time them.

She balked, her gaze locking on the yellow flag flapping offshore. For some reason, it looked a lot farther away than it had the day Jake and Jeremy had tested it out. "Jeremy…maybe you should just withdraw from the race."

Even as she spoke, Abby was adjusting the straps on a bright orange life jacket. Emma gasped when she felt Abby put it over her head and fasten the buckles around her waist.

"You know I don't like the water," she told her son in a terse whisper.

"You aren't going to be in the water," Jeremy said. "You're going to be on the raft."

"But what if we lose because of me?" A very real possibility, to Emma's way of thinking.

"That's okay." Jeremy tugged her toward the Team Victory flag stuck in the sand. The one that matched their T-shirts. "You and Jake said that doesn't matter. The important thing is to have fun, remember?"

Of course she remembered. But this wasn't exactly her idea of fun!

Emma looked over her shoulder, desperate to spot a familiar figure striding toward them. Tried to convince herself that Jake had somehow lost track of the time…

"Come on, Mom. It's going to start."

"Number four, Team Victory," the announcer called.

Heads swiveled in their direction.

"Team Victory," he repeated.

"Okay." She drew in a ragged breath. "Let's do it."

Jeremy raised his hand for a high five and Emma smacked her palm weakly against his.

The announcer read through the rules one more time. Emma's gaze traveled over the pieces of the raft and she tried to remember the order in which Jeremy and Jake had constructed it.

Where is he, God?

"Three…two…one." A whistle blew and Jeremy gave her a hammer.

Emma worked quickly, guided by memory and the occasional instruction from Jeremy. A few minutes later, she heard a splash as one of the rafts launched. Jeremy didn't spare a moment to glance up to see who was ahead of them.

"Ready." They pulled the raft across the narrow strip of sand. "You're going to have to paddle, Mom."

Emma summoned a smile. "It'll be fun."

Jeremy flashed a grin.

Even as Emma positioned herself on the raft, she looked around to see if Jake had arrived. Kate, Esther and Daniel stood next to Team Victory's flag, waving their arms and shouting out encouragements.

The raft dipped to accommodate their combined

weight and water flowed over the side. Emma gasped as it soaked through her clothing.

A collective groan rose from the group of onlookers as another raft capsized. A small row-boat immediately went to the contestants' aid.

They were in first place.

As they drew closer to the flag, Emma put her paddle across her lap. Her fingers trembled as she fumbled to untie one of the bright red bandanas from the buoy.

"I've got it. Let's go!" Emma shouted as soon as it was free.

As they turned the raft around, another one bumped up against them. The jolt pitched Jeremy to the side and Emma's heart followed suit.

She made a grab for his arm but he righted himself. "I'm okay," he gasped.

Paddling furiously, they passed several more rafts bobbing toward the flag. Some of the contestants lay on their stomachs, using their hands and feet to paddle.

As the cheering grew louder, it occurred to Emma that they were going to win.

"We have to tie the bandana to our flag," Jeremy said as the underside of the raft scraped against the sand. "Otherwise we're disqualified."

"I'll let you do the honors," Emma said. "You're faster than I am." And once the adrenaline wore off, she wasn't sure her legs would hold her upright!

They bailed off the side of the raft into the shallow water and dragged it onto shore. Jeremy sprinted ahead of her with the bandana.

Jeremy was knotting the bandana on their flag-pole as she reached his side. But the small group of people clustered around him weren't jumping up and cheering.

Emma's heart dropped like a stone when she saw Quinn standing next to Officer Koenigs. The man's ordinarily placid expression now reflected a grim resignation.

A sudden flashback weakened her knees.

She had seen that look before.

"First place goes to Team Victory," the announcer said. "Jeremy and Emma Barlow. Come over here and get your trophy."

"Jeremy—go get the trophy for us," Emma said hoarsely.

Fortunately, her son hadn't sensed anything amiss. With a grin, he loped over to the judge's stand.

Abby came alongside Emma and gave her arm a bracing squeeze.

Emma moistened her lips. Her gaze cut from Quinn back to Phil Koenigs. "What happened? Is it…Jake?"

The officer nodded reluctantly. "About six o'clock, the sheriff's department received a call that a vehicle in front of them was driving erratically. The caller followed the car until it turned off on a dead-end road about ten miles out of town." Phil paused and cleared his throat. "By the time the officer arrived on the scene, the occupants of the vehicle had gone into a cabin. He saw stolen property in the backseat of the car and called for backup."

"Why would Jake respond?" Emma stared at the older officer in confusion. Jake wasn't a county deputy, nor would a police chief be expected to respond to a routine call.

Unless it wasn't a routine call.

"Whoever was in the cabin shot at the officer," Phil explained. "For the last few hours, the officers have been in a standoff with the two men inside. Several departments in the area responded. From what we know, they're either drunk or strung out on drugs. I've been out of town the last few days visiting my daughter, but when I heard the call come over the radio, I drove back. I'd just stopped home to change into my uniform when Quinn tracked me down. He thought I should be the one to tell you what was going on so you'd hear the truth. Rumors are already starting to go around."

Most of the words filtered through Emma's mind. The ones that stayed turned her heart cold. *Shot at the officer. Strung out on drugs.*

"Thank you." Emma could feel a strange numbness seeping into every pore. The rushing sound in her ears made it difficult to concentrate on what the officer was saying.

"I have to get back there now," Phil told them. "Hopefully we'll get this thing wrapped up soon."

"We'll be praying for you and the other officers," Abby promised softly.

"I appreciate that, Miss Porter." Phil looked at Emma, his eyes dark with regret. "I'm sorry, Emma. I wish I didn't have to be the bearer of bad news."

Again.

The word hung in the air between them.

How could she have forgotten that this was what it had felt like? The uncertainty. The waiting. Living with the knowledge that at any moment, a situation could change. Your life could change.

"I appreciate you taking the time to come down and tell me." Emma reached out and shook his hand.

Phil nodded curtly. "I'm sure Jake will get word to you as soon as he can."

"Look at the trophy we won!" Jeremy skidded

up, holding a small gold trophy. His bright gaze searched the faces around him. "Is Jake here yet?"

Spots danced in front of Emma's eyes.

What was she going to tell her son?

"Not yet." Daniel answered the question. "Something came up this morning and he had to go to work."

"Work?" Jeremy's brow furrowed. "He's okay, though, isn't he?"

Emma swallowed hard. "I haven't heard from him yet." At least, Emma thought, she was telling the truth.

At the moment, she didn't dare consider the alternative.

"What a way to spend a day." Phil Koenigs leaned against the wall in the department break room, weariness etched in every line on his face. "Maureen will be glad when I call her and tell her to fire up the grill."

Steve Patterson shed his uniform shirt and draped it over a chair before casting a guilty look at Jake. "Sorry, Chief. No disrespect, but I'm beginning to offend myself."

"You were beginning to offend the rest of us, too," Trip muttered.

Jake listened to the officers, knowing the banter

was their way of releasing stress. The men had been strategically placed around the perimeter of the cabin, forced to remain nearly motionless in the hot sun for hours.

The call came in shortly after Jake's alarm had gone off that morning. Shots fired at a cabin north of Mirror Lake. With several county deputies on vacation, local departments had responded to the scene to help out. He got the directions from dispatch and called Emma on the way to the scene, sick at the thought of having to explain that he might not be there for the raft race.

The call had gone right to her voice mail and Jake hadn't had another opportunity to get in touch with her after that.

The standoff had lasted all day, until one of the young men had finally staggered out of the cabin shortly before dusk. He was worried about his friend, who'd been passed out for several hours.

He was taken into custody while the other man was transported to the hospital. Jake had remained at the scene until an inventory of the stolen property was completed and the car impounded.

The sheriff had contacted Jake after the young man gave a statement, letting him know that both men had been involved in the rash of cabin burglaries.

Jake was relieved it had turned out the way it did. Bad guys in custody—no one injured.

But would Emma see it that way?

Chapter Twenty-One

"I'm going to take Shadow for a walk, okay, Mom?" Jeremy appeared in the kitchen doorway.

"All right. I'm sure he'd like that." Emma forced a smile. She didn't blame her son for needing some time alone to think.

Once they had heard the news about Jake, neither one of them had felt like staying at the park for the rest of the celebration. Emma had done her best to hide her feelings from Jeremy, but he had been quiet on the drive back home, resistant to her attempts to draw him out.

She heard the front door close and laid her head on the table.

I don't understand, God.

The silent cry burst out of a place deep within her.

They'd gone through this before. By letting Jake

into their lives, she had put Jeremy in a situation where he could be hurt again. For six years, Emma had done everything within her power to protect her son...

She closed her eyes and drew in a ragged breath. Maybe that was the trouble. She had done everything in *her* power.

When I came to the end of my strength, I called out to God. He reached out His hand and He hasn't let go.

Jake's words. Said with absolute certainty.

Emma had always believed in God, but after Brian died, she had pulled away from Him, too.

She felt like that father in the story that Esther had told her. And she'd said that nothing in the heart was hidden from God, so Emma didn't bother to hold anything back this time. Even as she stumbled through the prayer, peace settled over her, a kind of peace she had never experienced before.

I'm here, God. And I'm reaching out to You. I'm tired of doing all of this alone. I need You. I want to trust You. Esther said that we can be honest with You, so here it is. I'm scared to death but I'm going to trust You. I'm going to trust that You're not going to let go of me, either.

"Mom?" Jeremy's soft voice intruded on her prayer. "You're crying."

"I'm praying." She sniffled.

"For Jake?"

"And for me."

The look of hope on her son's face was humbling. She drew him close.

"Do you mind if we pray together?" he asked.

"I think that's a great idea," Emma whispered.

They went into the living room and sat together on the couch, heads bowed, Shadow sprawled at their feet.

Jeremy's simple but heartfelt prayer struck a chord in Emma's heart.

"I know that Jake has to help people sometimes, God. That's his job. But me and mom are worried about him, so please keep him safe. Amen."

"Amen," Emma echoed.

The sound of a car coming up the driveway pushed them both to their feet. Jeremy raced to the window and brushed the curtain aside.

He twisted around to look at her. "I think it's Mr. Redstone."

Daniel?

Emma peered out the window and saw not one car, but three, lined up in the driveway. Behind the Redstones' pickup truck she recognized Abby's red convertible. Kate sat in the driver's seat of the vintage Thunderbird parked behind it.

By the time Emma reached the door, people were already filing in.

"We had all this leftover food," Abby informed her cheerfully. "So we thought we'd drop some off."

Daniel ruffled Jeremy's hair. "And I had to see the dog that Mrs. Peake has been talking about. He's a local celebrity."

"Shadow," Jeremy said.

Emma's throat swelled. No matter what they claimed their reasons were, she knew why they'd come.

When Brian died, people had reached out to her and she'd backed away.

This time, she opened the door wide and let them in.

Jake pulled into the driveway, surprised to see a line of cars parked in front of Emma's house.

After going home to shower and change his clothes, Jake had been tempted to crawl into bed, close his eyes and slip into oblivion for the next ten hours. But he couldn't. Not until he apologized to Jeremy. And to Emma.

The front door opened as Jake got out of the car and Jeremy hurtled toward him.

Jake didn't think twice. He caught the boy up in his arms and gave him a hard hug.

"You're okay," Jeremy gasped.

"I'm okay." Jake's heart wrenched. Until this moment, he wasn't sure if Jeremy would look at him with resentment for not being there when he needed him. "I'm sorry that I didn't make the race this morning, bud."

More sorry than he could say.

"I know you had to work. Officer Koenigs told us," Jeremy said, inadvertently twisting the knife in Jake's heart again.

He had talked with Phil several times over the course of the day, but the officer hadn't mentioned he was the one who had told Emma about the standoff.

Jake glanced toward the house. For all the cars, there were no signs of life. No sign of Emma, either.

Would she even want to see him?

"We won the race."

"What?" Jake dragged his gaze back to Jeremy's face.

"We won." Jeremy repeated the words with a proud grin.

Relief swept through Jake. Someone had come through for Jeremy when he hadn't been able to.

He sent up a silent thank you to the Lord looking out for him. "Who signed on as first mate? Was it Daniel? Quinn?"

"Nope. Mom did."

Jake couldn't have heard him right. "Your mom?"

"She was the only one who knew how to put the raft together," Jeremy reminded him. "She did good, even when I almost fell into the water when I was untying the bandana from the buoy."

If Jake had wondered if Emma would forgive him, Jeremy's matter-of-fact comment provided him with the answer.

Now he regretted giving in to the urge to kiss her even more. It only created another bond that had to be severed. Because if Emma ever did fall in love again, it wouldn't be with someone who brought pain and uncertainty back into her life.

"Do you want to see the trophy?" Jeremy was already tugging him toward the house.

"I don't want to intrude if you and your mom invited company over."

"We didn't invite them," Jeremy said blithely. "And it's just Mr. and Mrs. Redstone and Miss Porter and Kate."

Another twist of the knife.

If they had shown up without being invited, that meant they'd been worried about Emma, too.

* * *

"Quinn must be here." Abby rose to her feet when they heard a car door slam. "He said he was going to stop by after the park closed."

Emma hoped Abby's fiancé would have some word about Jake. As the day had stretched on, she had battled fear. Doubt. Familiar adversaries, only the difference was, she didn't feel as if she were facing them alone anymore.

At Daniel's suggestion, they had all prayed for Jake's safety and the safety of the other officers. After that, the man had proved to be a welcome distraction for Jeremy, taking him and Shadow on a long walk around the property.

Abby had taken over the kitchen, putting on a pot of coffee while Kate and Esther dished up plates of food. Their concern had wrapped around Emma like a warm blanket.

"I'll pour a cup of coffee for Quinn." Kate was on her way to the kitchen before Emma could stand up.

It was a good thing she wasn't standing.

Because the man Jeremy led into the living room wasn't Quinn O'Halloran. It was Jake.

Jake's heart stalled when he saw Emma.

Her face was pale. Her eyes red-rimmed and puffy.

He had done this to her.

"Praise God." Daniel clapped him on the back and everyone surrounded him. Everyone but Emma.

Jake hadn't expected to have an audience when he apologized to Emma, but maybe it was a blessing they weren't alone.

Kate herded him over to the sofa. "Tell us everything."

Not a chance, Jake thought. Instead, he briefly summarized the past fourteen hours, careful to gloss over certain details. Like the young man staggering out of the cabin with a loaded shotgun.

There was no point in putting that image in anyone's mind.

Fortunately, no one asked him to elaborate when he finished the story but Jake had no doubt that Emma, of all people, could fill in the details he had left out.

"I have to get something." Jeremy dashed out of the room and returned a few minutes later with a gold trophy.

"This is great." Jake summoned a smile as he took the trophy and turned it over in his hands. "I knew you could do it."

He tried to give it back but Jeremy shook his head.

"I want you to keep it."

"I can't do that. It belongs to you—and your mother." Jake couldn't look at Emma again. Not yet.

"But you helped me build the raft. You're part of Team Victory."

"But I wasn't there." Jake felt at a loss, knowing he didn't deserve something that meant so much to Jeremy.

"That's why I want you to have it. Mom said it's okay."

Jake felt as small as the gold letters stamped on the bottom of the trophy. "How about we make it a traveling trophy? I'll keep it for a month and then I'll give it back to you."

"And Mom can take it for a month, too."

"Right." Jake cleared his throat.

"Would you like a cup of coffee, Jake?" Kate waded bravely into the awkward silence that fell.

"Or something to eat?" Abby chimed in.

"No, thank you. I just stopped over to apologize to Jeremy and Emma for missing the race this morning." Jake backed toward the door. "I'm pretty exhausted."

Jeremy followed him to the door. "Are you coming over after church tomorrow?"

"I don't think I'll be able to." Jake pushed out a smile. "But I'll call you and we'll set something up, how's that?"

"Okay." Jeremy grinned. "Take good care of the trophy."

"I will."

At least that was one promise he could keep.

Emma looked out the window and saw Jake's car pull away.

For the past two weeks, he had followed the mentoring guidelines to the letter.

Once a week for four hours.

No more, no less.

School had started, so Jake had started to pick up Jeremy in the evening and take him into town or back to his cabin. If he did talk to her, he maintained a polite but careful distance.

It was driving Emma crazy.

Something had changed between them. The night of the parade, he had drawn her into his arms and kissed her. Now he treated her as if they were barely acquaintances.

More than anything, she wanted to tell him that she had surrendered her heart to the Lord. That she understood the freedom that came from trusting Him. In some ways, Emma felt as if she had come back to life again.

Did Jake realize that trusting her with his story had, in turn, helped her put her trust in God?

"Hi, Mom." Jeremy wandered in, lacking the

bounce Emma had gotten used to seeing after he spent time with Jake.

"Did you have fun?"

"Yeah."

"You don't sound too sure." Emma gave him a playful nudge. "What did you and Jake do tonight?"

"He helped me with my leaf collection for science class." Jeremy scuffed the toe of his tennis shoe against the concrete floor.

"You must have enjoyed that."

Jeremy shrugged. "I guess."

Emma put an empty mold into the sink and propped a hip against the table. "Want to tell me what's bothering you, sweetheart?"

"It's different now."

"What's different?"

"I like hanging out with Jake, but I liked it when he came over here, too."

So did Emma.

"Maybe you should tell him how you feel," she suggested cautiously.

"I did. He said that 'it's for the best.'" Jeremy knelt down and wrapped his arms around Shadow's neck. "But it doesn't feel like it's for the best."

Emma frowned. What had Jake meant by that? The best for whom?

"I'm going inside to work on the rest of my

homework." Jeremy rose to his feet. "Come on, Shadow."

Tears pricked Emma's eyes. Not just for Jeremy, but for both of them.

Whatever his reason, Jake had walked away. Emma decided it was time to find out why.

Chapter Twenty-Two

Jake glanced at his watch. If Matt didn't show up at the pavilion in five minutes, he was going back to the police department.

Maybe he would cut it down to three minutes.

The pastor had called earlier that morning and said he wanted to talk to him, but for some odd reason, had suggested they meet at the park instead of the church office.

Because Jake had a pretty good idea what the topic would be, he was reluctant to meet with Matt at all.

The night before, when he had dropped Jeremy off and saw the lights on in Emma's workroom, it had taken all his self-control to drive away. And it hadn't helped that Jeremy had asked him why they no longer spent any time at his house—and why they were only getting together once a week.

Jake had given him a vague answer about school

starting and it being for the best, but the truth was, it was killing him to stay away from Emma and cut down on the amount of time he spent with Jeremy.

He sat down on one of the benches overlooking the water and tried to pray. Lately, Jake's conversations with God had been a struggle, too.

"I'm surprised you're still here." Matt jogged up to him.

"You had another two minutes and twelve seconds."

The pastor smiled, but it didn't quite reach his eyes. "I believe you."

"So what's on your mind?"

"Skipping the small talk, huh?" Matt shook his head. "I'm all for that—what's going on with you and the Barlows?"

Maybe he would rather discuss the weather, Jake thought. But it was too late now.

"Did Jeremy talk to you?"

"Actually, I got a call from your brother."

"You talked to Andy?" Jake lifted a skeptical brow.

"That's right. He's concerned about you. And so am I," Matt added.

Unbelievable, Jake thought. Or maybe not, considering what his brother and his friend did for a living. "I'm a big boy. I don't need you guys hovering around me like I'm a five-year-old learning to ride a bicycle."

"Hovering?" Matt snorted. "We were arguing on the phone about which one of us gets to do the honor of smacking you upside the head."

"I didn't make this decision lightly," Jake growled. If anything, it was killing him. Over the past week, he'd been careful to stick to the four-hour time block he'd agreed to upon joining the mentoring program.

"Why *did* you make it?"

Jake couldn't believe he had to ask. He plowed his fingers through his hair and speared Matt with a look. "You know why."

"Humor me."

"I saw Emma's face that day. It was like sending her back in time to the day Brian died, right down to Phil Koenigs giving her the news." Even now, Jake's composure staggered under the weight of it. "For a while, I thought there could be something between us—something good—but I can't promise her that I'll always be safe. That I'll always come home on time or…that I'll come home at all. I'm not going to put her and Jeremy through that again."

"Are you sure that Emma is the one you're protecting?" Matt asked quietly. "Or are you protecting yourself?"

"Maybe I'm protecting all of us." Jake stared at the water with unseeing eyes. Even if Emma shared his feelings, he couldn't stand it if, down the road, those feelings changed. Better to make a clean break now. "This is for the best."

"If you're making a decision about us, don't I have a say in what's best?"

Jake froze at the sound of Emma's voice.

He shot an accusing look at Matt, who shrugged. Not at all repentant—or surprised—that Emma was there. That she might have overheard some of their conversation.

"What happened to confidential meetings with the pastor?" he muttered.

"Oh, those take place in my office," Matt said with cheerful disregard for the dark look Jake tossed his way. "The park is open to the public. I have no control over who comes and goes. And if you'll excuse me, I'm going."

Jake's mouth dropped open, but he couldn't get a word out. Not that it would have mattered. Matt was already halfway to the car.

"Jake?"

He couldn't look at her. It *hurt* to look at her.

"I should be used to being set up by my friends." Self-preservation sharpened his tone.

Emma flinched and guilt arrowed through him. This wasn't her fault, Jake reminded himself.

"Don't be upset with Pastor Wilde. I called the church this morning and asked if I could set up an appointment to talk to him. He said he wouldn't be able to see me until this afternoon, because the two of you were meeting."

"At the park."

"He might have mentioned that, too." Emma took a step closer.

Jake couldn't help it. He braced himself to absorb the pain and looked at her now. The luminous smile on her face stole his breath.

"How much did you hear?"

"Enough to know that you're wrong."

"Am I?" Jake's lips twisted. "So you weren't upset with me for standing Jeremy up on the day of the race? Resentful that I had to put my job ahead of him? Worried about me when you found out that I was in a standoff with a drunk kid holding a shotgun?"

"You're right." Emma's voice trembled. "I was all those things. At first. But the thing you are wrong about was that you put me in a situation I'd been in before. I wasn't. And that *was* your fault. Because of you, I didn't go back to that place because I'm not the same person I was six years ago. I'm not the same person I was a month ago. I wasn't, what your verse says, *rooted in love*. I didn't trust God—now I do. I know He'll never leave me.

"You told me that spending time with Jeremy was a gift that you didn't deserve, but you didn't see that you are as much of a gift to us. To *me*. You questioned whether you had anything to give but you gave me something that I'd lost. Hope."

Emma searched Jake's eyes, looking for a sign that something she'd said had made a difference. Made him change his mind.

She hadn't meant to eavesdrop on his conversation with Pastor Wilde, but when she'd heard the anguish and regret in Jake's voice, she hadn't been able to take another step forward.

Was it possible he didn't realize what he had brought to their lives?

He had pulled away from her and Jeremy, not because his feelings had changed, but in order to protect them from pain.

"I'm afraid," Jake said flatly. "Afraid that I'll let you down. Afraid that I don't know enough about raising kids or about making you happy. About not being what you and Jeremy need. I told you I was new at all this."

He started to move away, but she caught his hand.

"It feels new to me, too," she admitted. "I told you the truth when I said I'm not the same person.

We're going to make mistakes, but I think…I think if we both stay close to God, nothing will come between us."

Jake pulled her against him and buried his face in her hair. "I love you, Emma."

She clung to him, absorbing the words like summer rain. "I love you, too."

"I'll admit I've been afraid of something else."

"What?"

The flecks of gold in his eyes sent a shiver of heat rippling through her. "I've been afraid to kiss you again."

"I've heard you aren't supposed to let fear stop you from doing the things you want to do," Emma said a little breathlessly.

Jake smiled that heart-stopping smile as he drew her closer. His lips took hers in a searching kiss and Emma melted against him, this time telling him without words how she felt about him.

When they broke apart a few minutes later, Jake stared down at her, a dazed expression on his face. "Thank you for helping me overcome my fear."

"I'm just returning the favor, Chief Sutton." Emma leaned against his broad chest, pressing her face against his heart.

His arms tightened around her. "You're the brave one. I was ready to walk away."

"You wouldn't have gotten very far." Emma chuckled. "If I had to, I was going to remind you that you had a week left on our trial period."

"Are you saying that you want to extend it?"

The teasing look on his face made Emma respond in kind. She pretended to consider the question. "I think we should. How long do you think it should be this time?"

Jake drew her back into his arms. "I was thinking maybe...forever?"

"What a coincidence." Emma smiled up into his eyes. "That's exactly what I was thinking."

Epilogue

"You look kind of nervous, Jake." Jeremy tipped his head as Jake paced the floor in front of him.

"I need to talk to you about something."

"Okay." Jeremy leaned back against the sofa cushions. "Go for it."

Go for it.

Those three little words were the reason he was so nervous in the first place.

"All right." Jake took a deep breath. "I want to marry your mom," he said. "But before I ask her, I have to know how you feel about it."

Jeremy folded his arms across his chest.

Okay, so Jake had been half hoping he would leap off the sofa and give him a high five. Shake his hand. *Something.* But one of the things he loved about the kid was the way he approached everything—from breakfast cereal to a proposal of marriage—with thoughtful concentration.

"You better sit down, Jake."

Jake sat.

"If you and Mom got married, where would we live?"

"Well, your mother will have something to say about that, of course, but I thought we might want to stay here. You have your room fixed up the way you want it here and Shadow has space to run. We could fix up the barn and turn it into a studio for your mom, especially now that Abby talked her into teaching classes for the people who stay at the inn."

"And the apple tree is here," Jeremy added.

The apple tree.

Jake thought back to the first time he had met Emma. When she had opened the door, he had had no idea his life was about to change. No idea that he had been coming *home*.

God, You are so amazing.

"That's another thing." Jake felt his throat tighten. "Your dad loved you and your mom very much and I'm not trying to take his place. I don't want you to forget him...but I hope we can add new memories to the ones you have."

"Are you going to have more kids?"

"I don't know." Jake slumped back against the cushion, trying to hide the fact that the innocent question had turned his bones to liquid. "Your mom and I haven't talked about…adding on to the family. But how would you feel about it? A brother or sister?"

Or, Jake warmed to the idea, maybe one—or two—of each.

"I think it would be cool—as long as I don't have to share my room if it's a sister."

"Sisters in the spare bedroom. Promise."

Jeremy was silent for a few minutes and Jake could almost see the wheels turning in his head.

"Do you have a ring?"

Jake hid a smile.

"As a matter of fact, I do." In his pocket, waiting for the right moment to slip it on Emma's finger.

Jeremy held out his hand.

"Oh. You want to take a look at it." Jake fumbled in his pocket and retrieved the tiny velvet box. He presented it to Jeremy.

"It's a good one." Jeremy pronounced after inspecting it carefully. "Mom will like it."

Jake hoped so. He had purchased the ring a week ago, hoping that Emma would understand the significance of the slender gold band set with three diamonds—one for each of them.

"So, what do you think?"

When Jeremy didn't respond right away, Jake felt a pang of concern.

"Jeremy, I can't promise that I won't make

mistakes," he said quietly. "But I love your mom… and I love you, too. I believe that God wants us to be family."

"I know." Jeremy looked down at his hands.

"You have another question, I can tell. You never have to be afraid to tell me what's on your mind. Go ahead and ask me."

"After you and mom get married, do you mind if I call you Dad instead of Jake?"

Jake's vision blurred. "I would love that."

Jeremy grinned.

"So…" Jake's self-control finally buckled under the pressure. "Does that mean I have your blessing?"

"Yup—"

The front door opened and they heard Emma call out a cheerful hello. A second later she appeared in the doorway.

"What's going on in here?"

Jake couldn't answer. As usual, seeing Emma took his breath away. In the past few weeks he had seen a transformation in her that he could only attribute to the Lord. The grief had thawed, leaving behind a radiant warmth in her eyes.

"We're having a talk," Jeremy said smugly.

"A talk? That sounds serious." Emma breezed into the room, depositing purse and keys on the table near the door. She leaned over and squeezed Jake's hand. "What about?"

"I'm going to bed now." Jeremy launched himself off the sofa. "Jake will tell you. Maybe you guys should take Shadow for a walk. There's a full moon tonight."

"Thanks, Jeremy. I'll take it from here," Jake whispered.

A full moon? And take what from here?

Emma looked at Jake, puzzled, but he merely shrugged.

They were both acting strange.

"I'll be up to pray with you in a few minutes." Emma dropped a kiss on her son's head.

Jake held out her jacket and she slipped it on, resisting the urge to turn into his arms and not let go.

"Come on. We don't want to miss that full moon," he said.

Shadow disappeared ahead of them into the shadows.

"How did everything go tonight?" Jake took her hand and the warmth of his skin chased away the chill in the October air.

"Esther is convinced she can teach me to knit but I think I'll stick to mosaics." Emma chuckled as she remembered her first attempt that evening when she joined the Knit-Our-Hearts-Together group. "Kate almost gave up, too. She said something about using her knitting needles as plant stakes."

When Jake didn't smile, Emma stopped and planted her hands on her hips. "All right, what's going on? Is it something with Jeremy? You two looked pretty serious when I walked in. What were you talking about?"

Jake's silence—and the fact that he withdrew his hand from hers—added to Emma's concern.

"We were talking about this," he finally said.

Emma glanced down and saw the velvet box cradled in Jake's palm. The light from the porch illuminated the diamond ring in the center of it.

"I love you, Emma. Will you marry me?"

Emma stared down at the ring, overwhelmed by love for the man standing in front of her. She'd sensed that Jake was taking things slowly out of respect for her but Emma was ready to start their life together. She'd even confided to Kate and Abby that if he didn't propose soon, she was going to have to propose to *him*.

"Jake—"

Emma paused as the front door opened and light spilled across the yard.

"Well?" Jeremy peered at them from the doorway. "What did she say?"

Emma started to laugh and Jake smiled.

"Well? What did she say?" he whispered.

Emma smiled up at him.

"She said *yes*."

* * * * *

Dear Reader,

I hope you enjoyed getting to know Emma and Jake (and, of course, Jeremy and Shadow!) during your second visit to Mirror Lake.

As a police officer's wife, I know it isn't always easy to send my husband off to work every day, not knowing what situations he will have to face. Like Emma, I've learned that staying close to God and trusting Him brings peace. I hope you have found the same, no matter what your circumstances.

In the next book, Matthew Wilde's life is turned upside down when a "black sheep" wanders into the fold. Everyone is talking about Zoey Decker... but will the pastor listen to gossip—or his heart—when it comes to Mirror Lake's prodigal daughter? You'll have to plan another visit to find out!

I love to hear from you! Please visit my Web site at www.kathrynspringer.com and sign up for my quarterly newsletter.

Blessings,

Kathryn Springer

QUESTIONS FOR DISCUSSION

1. Why is Emma's response negative when Jake shows up with an apple tree rather than flowers on the anniversary of her husband's death? What is the underlying reason for that response?

2. Both Jake and Emma went through a traumatic event that changed their lives. What were the differences in the way they perceived God afterward?

3. Why is Emma opposed to her son having a mentor? Do you feel that her concerns are valid? Why or why not?

4. Jake doubts that he has anything to offer a boy Jeremy's age, yet he agrees to become his mentor because he feels that God is leading him in that direction. Have you ever been in a similar situation? Describe the outcome.

5. How much of a role do you think Emma's childhood plays in her hesitation to reach out to the people in Mirror Lake?

6. Kate tells Jake that people left Emma alone after Brian's death out of respect for her privacy, but questions whether they did the right thing. Have you ever hesitated to reach out to a grieving friend? Why?

7. Emma tells people that her mosaic work is just a hobby, but Esther Redstone sees it as more than that. What do you think about the older woman's insight about "broken things" that God can use to make something beautiful?

8. Do you have a special hobby or interest? What is it?

9. Jeremy's childlike faith encourages Emma to begin seeking God again. Has a family member ever done the same for you? In what way?

10. There are many times that police officers and firefighters must put emergencies before other obligations. How do you feel about that? What was your reaction when Jake couldn't participate in the raft race?

11. Jake has deep feelings for Emma, yet he is the one who steps back from the relationship after

Reflection Days. Why? Do you understand/ agree with his decision?

12. What character in the book can you most relate to? Why?

13. What was your favorite scene in the book? Why?

14. In what ways do Jake's and Emma's personalities complement each other?

15. Emma tells Jake that she isn't the same person she was when Brian died. Why? What do you think that means in terms of her ability to open her heart to love again?

16. Read Ephesians 3:16–19 and take some time to reflect on the passage. What do you think it means to be "rooted and established in love"?

LARGER-PRINT BOOKS!

**GET 2 FREE
LARGER-PRINT NOVELS
PLUS 2 FREE
MYSTERY GIFTS**

Larger-print novels are now available...

YES! Please send me 2 FREE LARGER-PRINT Love Inspired® novels and my 2 FREE mystery gifts (gifts are worth about $10). After receiving them, if I don't wish to receive any more books, I can return the shipping statement marked "cancel". If I don't cancel, I will receive 6 brand-new novels every month and be billed just $4.74 per book in the U.S. or $5.24 per book in Canada. That's a saving of over 20% off the cover price. It's quite a bargain! Shipping and handling is just 50¢ per book.* I understand that accepting the 2 free books and gifts places me under no obligation to buy anything. I can always return a shipment and cancel at any time. Even if I never buy another book, the two free books and gifts are mine to keep forever.

122/322 IDN E7QP

Name _____ (PLEASE PRINT) _____

Address _____ Apt. # _____

City _____ State/Prov. _____ Zip/Postal Code _____

Signature (if under 18, a parent or guardian must sign) _____

Mail to **Steeple Hill Reader Service:**

IN U.S.A.: P.O. Box 1867, Buffalo, NY 14240-1867
IN CANADA: P.O. Box 609, Fort Erie, Ontario L2A 5X3

Not valid to current subscribers to Love Inspired Larger-Print books.

**Are you a current subscriber to Love Inspired books
and want to receive the larger-print edition?
Call 1-800-873-8635 or visit www.morefreebooks.com.**

* Terms and prices subject to change without notice. Prices do not include applicable taxes. Sales tax applicable in N.Y. Canadian residents will be charged applicable provincial taxes and GST. Offer not valid in Quebec. This offer is limited to one order per household. All orders subject to approval. Credit or debit balances in a customer's account(s) may be offset by any other outstanding balance owed by or to the customer. Please allow 4 to 6 weeks for delivery. Offer available while quantities last.

Love Inspired HISTORICAL

INSPIRATIONAL HISTORICAL ROMANCE

Engaging stories of romance,
adventure and faith,
these novels are set in
various historical periods
from biblical times
to World War II.

NOW AVAILABLE!

Steeple
Hill®